Never Like My Father

Childhood Trauma, Family Addiction, and One Sacred Promise

Howard Kane

Hidden Alpha Capital LLC

About the author

Howard Kane writes the stories most people are afraid to tell.

As a former Fortune 500 executive, he knows what it feels like to appear successful on the outside while quietly unraveling on the inside. For years, he hid his drinking behind late nights, busy calendars, and a polished smile. When he finally faced the truth about his addiction, he discovered that recovery wasn't just possible; it was life-changing.

Howard channels that experience into memoir-style novels that explore addiction, family trauma, money, and power. His five-book saga, ***The Daughter of a Drunk***, follows Olivia Parker from a terrified little girl in a small Ohio town, vowing she'll never be like her father, to a woman fighting billionaires, corrupt institutions, and her own worst impulses. Beginning with ***Never Like My Father***, the series blends coming-of-age drama, generational alcoholism, and high-stakes whistleblower suspense into one continuous, bingeable story.

He also writes standalone novels rooted in alcohol dependence and recovery, including ***The Double Life of a High-Functioning Alcoholic***, which pulls back the curtain on the addiction that hides behind ambition and success, and ***From Wine Mom to Sober Mom***, which shines a light on the unique struggles mothers face when drinking threatens everything they love.

Through raw honesty and lived experience, Howard's books show that surviving a drunk parent or being the drunk parent is only the beginning. The real story is what you do with the wreckage. Readers describe his work as "impossible to put down" because the characters feel uncomfortably real, and their choices never come cheap.

If you've ever questioned your relationship with drinking, grown up in the shadow of someone else's, or wondered how far you'd go to protect the people you love, Howard Kane's stories are for you.

Website: https://selfcarejourneybooks.com/

Contents

Chapter One

The Bathroom Floor Vow

"DEAR GOD, I WILL never, ever, EVER be like my father. I will never drink. I will never hurt people. I will never make my children scared. I promise. Amen."

I was six years old, on my knees on the cold bathroom floor. The linoleum pressed into my skin. My hands were tightly clasped together, just like I'd seen people do in church.

The air was thick with the sour smell of Jack Daniel's and vomit. It burned my nose and twisted my stomach. Behind me, Daddy's body finally stopped shaking after what felt like forever. Twenty minutes, maybe more. I thought he might really die right there.

It was Easter Sunday, 1999.

I didn't know it yet, but this morning was going to live inside me forever.

Just minutes earlier, I had been walking down the hallway in my duck pajamas. Mommy bought them especially for Easter, little yellow ducks all over soft white cotton. I wanted Daddy to see me in them because he always made funny faces when I wore something new and cute. I wanted that smile.

But instead of a smile, I found him on the bathroom floor.

Bob Parker. My daddy. Six feet tall, two hundred pounds, the man who had carried me on his shoulders at the fair. Now he was a heap of sweat and whiskey and sounds I didn't have names for yet. His dark hair stuck flat to his forehead. His blue work shirt, the one from McDonald's yesterday, was soaked with vomit and Jack Daniel's.

His body shook like he was freezing, even though it wasn't cold in Ohio in April. I stood in the doorway, my heart pounding.

"Daddy?" I whispered.

His eyes were open, but they weren't his. They looked empty, as if someone had turned him off inside.

Not the daddy who read "Green Eggs and Ham" with silly voices. Not the daddy who laughed so big when I squealed at the rides last summer.

This was the Jack Daniel's daddy. The poison one.

From down the hall, I could hear Mommy crying softly. The kind of crying that tried to hide from me and Leo. From our room came Leo's little whimper. He was probably under his blanket with Rex, his green dinosaur. That was his safe place. At four years old, he already knew how to hide when things got bad. I wished I could hide too.

But someone had to take care of Daddy.

I grabbed the blue washcloth from the towel rack. I dipped it in cold water and wiped his face. The vomit came off in streaks, running down into the sink in colors I didn't want to see. I wiped his neck and hands. I wanted him to look like my daddy again, not this broken man on the floor.

And the whole time, I thought about Thursday.

Thursday night, when he had been mine again. My real daddy.

"Come here, princess," he'd said, patting his lap in the big brown recliner. His voice was warm. He smelled like Old Spice and coffee, and something else that was just him. I curled into his chest, the safest place in the world.

"What should we read tonight?"

"Green Eggs and Ham!" I'd yelled because it was my favorite. He grinned like he already knew.

He opened the book like it was a big show. "That Sam-I-Am!" he said in a grumpy, funny voice. "That Sam-I-Am! I do not like that Sam-I-Am!"

I giggled so hard I had to press my belly. His eyes twinkled when he looked at me. The same blue as mine.

"See, princess? Sometimes the things we think we won't like turn out to be wonderful surprises."

"Like what?"

"Like Brussels sprouts," he said. "Or like being a daddy. I thought it would be scary, but then you came, and it was the best thing ever."

He kissed my head, and I believed him. I felt so safe, so loved.

Three days later, here we were. He was the scary thing.

When I finished cleaning him, I pulled back into the corner where I always said my bedtime prayers. My knees hit the cold floor, and my hands folded together again. But this time wasn't about "God bless Mommy, Daddy, and Leo." This was different.

"I will never be like my father," I whispered, then louder, until it felt like the words filled the room. Each time I said it, it felt more real. Like carving something into stone. Like daring the future not to mess with me.

Behind me, his breathing grew steadier, but it still rattled. The sound of a fight he was losing.

I looked at him one last time. Propped against the bathtub, head heavy, shirt stained, the smell of whiskey sticking to everything, even me. My duck pajamas smelled like him now. The bad him. The kind I wanted to run away from forever.

"Olivia?" Mommy's voice came softly from the hall.

"Coming, Mommy."

I took one more look. I knew I had to remember this, even though I hated it. This was the proof. This was why I could never touch alcohol. Because if I did, I might turn into him.

The rest of Easter Sunday moved in that hushed way our crisis days always did. Mommy made scrambled eggs and toast, acting like everything was normal. Her smile was too bright, as if it hurt her face to keep it there.

Leo sat in front of the TV, Rex tucked under his arm, eating slowly. He kept glancing at the hallway where Daddy's door stayed closed. His little fingers rubbed the dinosaur's tail again and again.

We were supposed to be at church. Mommy had laid out my yellow dress the night before, the one with tiny white flowers. She had even bought me white shoes with shiny buckles that clicked on the floor. I had wanted to wear them. Instead, I sat at the kitchen table in my duck pajamas, picking at eggs I didn't want to eat.

"When's Daddy gonna wake up?" Leo asked, his voice thick and tired.

"Daddy's resting, sweetie," Mommy said. Her voice was bright in that fake way I already knew meant she was scared. "He came down with a bad stomach flu. He needs lots of sleep."

I wanted to tell her she was wrong. Flu didn't smell like Jack Daniel's. Flu didn't make someone shake and breathe like that. But I didn't have words for what was really wrong, so I just nodded and ate a bite of egg.

Around eleven, the phone rang.

"Linda?" Mrs. Willson's voice was bright, full of Sunday church energy. "We missed you folks at service. Pastor Williams asked me to check. Is everything alright?"

I watched Mommy's shoulders go stiff. She looked toward the hallway, then forced her voice into something soft and almost normal.

"Oh, hi Betty. Yes, we're fine. Bob came down with something awful yesterday. We think it's the stomach flu. Didn't want to risk spreading it."

"Oh, my stars. On Easter Sunday, too. You tell him we're praying. And if you need anything, anything at all, you call me."

"That's so kind, thank you."

When Mommy hung up, she leaned against the counter. Her eyes closed. I could see her lips moving, counting to ten under her breath. She only did that when she was trying not to cry.

Three more calls came. Each time she said the same lie. Stomach flu. Sudden. Up all night. By the last call, she almost sounded like she believed it.

After lunch, Mommy washed dishes that were already clean. Leo curled up on the couch with Rex, asleep. I slipped out the back door.

The yard was small, just a patch of grass, the oak tree in the corner, and Mommy's garden along the fence. The air smelled like dirt and new leaves. It smelled clean. Not like the house. Not like whiskey.

That's when I saw the rabbit.

It lay under the oak, small and brown with white spots near its nose. At first, I thought it was sleeping. But it wasn't. Its eyes were closed, and it didn't move at all.

I had never seen something dead before. Not this close.

I sat in the grass, careful not to touch it. Its fur looked soft, almost like Rex's belly. But Rex was warm when you hugged him. This rabbit looked cold.

"Are you okay?" I whispered, even though I knew it couldn't hear.

I thought about Daddy that morning, the way his body went still after all the shaking. For a second, I thought maybe he was gone, like this rabbit. Then he had started breathing again.

"I'm sorry you're dead," I told the rabbit. "I'm sorry something bad happened to you."

The wind moved the leaves above me, making a whispering sound. For a moment, I almost believed the rabbit was answering.

"I made a promise to God today," I said softly, like I was telling a secret. "I promised I'll never be like Daddy when he's sick. I promised I'll be good."

I picked a dandelion and laid it next to the rabbit, like people bring flowers to a hospital bed.

"You can help me remember," I said. "You can help me keep my promise."

The rabbit stayed quiet and still. That felt safe somehow. Promises were better when given to someone who couldn't tell.

When I came back inside, the house was quiet in a careful way. The kind of quiet that meant Daddy was awake, but everyone was pretending he wasn't. I heard the TV low in their room and the sound of someone moving slowly, trying not to be noticed.

"Where were you, baby?" Mommy asked. She stood at the sink, her hands in soapy water, scrubbing a plate that was already clean.

"Outside. I found a dead rabbit under the tree."

Her hands froze. "Oh. That's very sad, isn't it?"

"Yeah. But it looked like it wasn't hurting anymore."

She turned, her green eyes watching me closely. They looked worried, soft, and careful all at once.

"Are you okay, Olivia? About this morning. About Daddy being sick?"

I nodded quickly. "I'm fine, Mommy. I'm always fine."

And I meant it.

She looked at me a moment longer, then turned back to the dishes.

The afternoon moved slowly and quietly, the kind of quiet that always followed a bad morning. Leo woke up from his nap and dumped his Legos across the carpet. He built tall towers and little houses, talking to Rex about which spots were the safest to hide in. Mommy started dinner, pot roast with carrots and potatoes, the kind of meal that tried to say everything was fine, even when it wasn't.

I sat at the kitchen table with my coloring book, pressing hard with my crayons. My mind kept drifting back to promises and rabbits and the two different daddies I knew. The one who read me stories and called me princess. And the one who shook so hard on the bathroom floor that I thought he might stop breathing.

Around six, I heard movement from their bedroom: heavy footsteps, the bathroom door closing, water running. Normal sounds, but my stomach still tightened. I wasn't scared he'd hit us; he never did, but I didn't know which version of him was coming out: the soft story reader or the stranger who made me want to hide like Leo.

Twenty minutes later, the door opened.

Daddy stepped into the hallway, and I let out a breath I didn't know I'd been holding. His hair was combed, his face shaved. He wore clean jeans and his Cleveland Browns t-shirt. He smelled like Old Spice and soap, almost like the real Daddy again.

"Hey there, princess," he said when he saw me at the table. His voice was rough and scratchy, but gentle.

"Hi, Daddy."

He walked over and knelt down beside me so we were eye level. Up close, I could see the red in his eyes and his pale skin, but he was smiling, or at least trying to.

"I'm sorry about this morning, princess. Daddy wasn't feeling good. I know it was scary for you."

I nodded. My throat felt too tight for words.

"But I'm better now. Much better." He touched my cheek with his big hand, the same hand that had been shaking so violently on the bathroom floor. Now it was steady, warm, safe. For a moment, it felt like nothing bad had ever happened.

"You know you're my good girl, right? My very, very good girl?"

I nodded again. My chest swelled. This was the Daddy I wanted to keep forever.

"I love you, Daddy."

"I love you too, princess. More than all the stars in the sky."

That was our special phrase. He had said it since I was little, and I used to believe it was true, every single star. But tonight, his words felt heavier, as if he was trying to convince himself as much as me.

He pulled me into a hug. His arms were strong and gentle, and I pressed my face against his shirt. That's when I smelled it. Under the Old Spice, under the soap and toothpaste, there was still a thin line of whiskey on his breath. Not much, but enough to remind me.

The promise I made that morning burned stronger in me. Daddy's hug was soft and warm, but the smell told me the danger was still there. Love and poison all mixed together.

"You're going to be amazing, Olivia," he whispered into my hair. His voice sounded thick, heavy with something I couldn't name then. Maybe guilt. Maybe love. Maybe both. "Better than amazing. You're going to be everything I never was."

I hugged him tighter, breathing in the mix of Old Spice and whiskey. It was confusing. I loved him so much it hurt, even when he scared me, even when he made Mommy cry and Leo hide. That love made everything harder to understand.

He kissed my forehead, then went back into the bedroom. I heard the sharp sound of a beer can opening. The sound landed in my stomach like a stone.

I changed into my yellow duck pajamas and crawled into bed. I pulled the blankets up under my chin. Across the room, I could hear Leo breathing softly and steadily, lost in his little-boy dreams.

I closed my eyes and whispered my promise again.

"I will never be like my father. I will never drink like him. Never. I won't hurt people or make my kids scared the way he scares us."

The words felt big in the dark, like magic. I pressed my hands together as if I were still praying.

"Never, never, never," I whispered.

Outside, the rain began to fall on the sidewalks of Millfield. In the kitchen, Mommy cleaned the dishes with slow, careful sounds. From the bedroom, I thought I heard another beer open.

I squeezed my eyes shut and held my promise close, as if it could keep me safe.

Chapter Two

Reading the Footsteps

FALL 2001

"Listen, Leo. Can you hear the difference?"

I was eight, crouched in the narrow hallway, showing my six-year-old brother the most important lesson we had: how to read Daddy's footsteps the way other kids read the weather.

"That's regular walking," I whispered, moving my feet across the worn carpet, light and even. "That means Daddy's okay."

Leo nodded hard, his blue eyes locked on my face. Same as mine. Same as Daddy's when they're clear. He looked like he was studying for a test he couldn't afford to fail.

"Now listen to this." I stomped heavier, dragging my steps, letting them wobble. "That's danger. Heavy and uneven, like he's walking through water. That means hide."

"Hide where?" Leo asked.

"Anywhere you can. Under the table. In your room. But the best spot is the basement. Behind the big boxes. Remember where I showed you?"

"B-behind the boxes?" His stutter came out, the one that had started over the summer. It slipped into his words when he was scared, when he was too tired, or when Daddy had been drinking too many nights in a row. Mommy said it was normal, that kids outgrew those things. But I knew better. I knew exactly when it started.

The night Daddy shoved Mommy so hard she hit the kitchen counter and couldn't hide the bruises.

"That's right," I told him. "Behind the boxes. And if you hear the heavy footsteps, you run there and wait for me. Don't come out until I come get you."

"What if you d-don't come?"

The question made my stomach twist. What if Daddy hurt me too much to go get him? What if something happened worse than anything we'd seen yet?

"I'll always come," I said. I made my voice sound strong, even though inside I wasn't sure. "That's what big sisters do. They always come."

Leo smiled a little then. For a moment, he looked like a regular six-year-old kid, not one who needed escape plans in his own house.

"Now you practice," I said. "Show me the footsteps."

We spent ten minutes pacing the hallway, trading safe and danger steps. Leo got good at it quickly. By the time Mommy called us for dinner, he could tell Daddy's drinking walk from three rooms away.

It wasn't a thing kids should have to learn. But for us, it was survival.

Dinner started calmly that night. Daddy was on day two without drinking, which meant he was trying hard to be good. That morning he'd made Mickey Mouse pancakes, with blueberries for eyes and a strawberry smile. Leo clapped his hands and giggled, and for twenty minutes, our kitchen felt like something from a TV commercial.

Now, Daddy cut his meat into perfect squares, careful and neat. He asked about school, listening closely, his eyes clear. He laughed at Leo's story about a frog at recess. He told

Mommy the meatloaf was the best he'd ever had, his voice warm, like maybe he truly believed it.

"How was school today, princess?" he asked me.

"Good," I said. "Mrs. Morales said I'm reading at a fifth-grade level."

"That's my smart girl," he said, pride shining in his eyes. The real pride. This was the Daddy who taught me to throw a baseball, who spent a whole Saturday building a birdhouse with me. It still sat in the backyard, even though no birds ever came. Proof that sometimes we could make beautiful things together.

"Leo's smart too," I said quickly because I had learned Daddy sometimes forgot about him. "He can count to a hundred."

"That's right, I can!" Leo shouted and started counting right there at the table. "One, two, three, four, five..."

Daddy laughed, the real laugh. "That's great, buddy. Next week we'll go for two hundred."

For half an hour, we were a normal family. Daddy asked questions, Mommy told stories from the diner, and Leo made silly jokes that weren't funny but made us laugh anyway.

And for a little while, I almost believed it could stay that way.

Then, Daddy went into the kitchen for another beer. His third that night. A few seconds later, I heard the sound that always meant trouble.

The bottle hitting the trash can.

Not the careful clink that said he was done. This was the angry crash of glass against metal, the sound of someone running out of what he needed.

"Linda," Daddy called, his voice already sharper. "Where's the other six-pack?"

"That was the last of it, Bob," Mommy said, her voice careful and steady. "I thought you were just having a couple with dinner."

"A couple? It's been a long day, Linda. A long week. I think I deserve more than a couple."

Here it came. The change. The storm rolling in. You could see it from far away, but there was never anything you could do to stop it.

I looked at Leo. His fork was frozen above his plate. His face was pale. Rex sat in his lap like always, the one thing he never let go of when Daddy was drinking.

"Bob, you've already had three—"

"Don't tell me what I've had." His voice cut through hers like a blade. "I work forty hours a week at that goddamn plant.

I pay for this house. I pay for this food. I can decide how many beers I drink."

"I wasn't trying to—"

"Yes, you were. You were trying to manage me. Like I'm one of the kids. Like I can't make my own decisions."

That's when the footsteps started. Heavy. Uneven. Pacing from the kitchen to the living room and back. The danger footsteps Leo and I had practiced in the hallway.

I caught Leo's eyes and nodded toward the basement. Time to go.

But before we could move, Daddy came into the dining room doorway. His face had changed. Ten minutes ago, he'd been laughing. Now his eyes were cold, his fists tight.

"You know what I think, Linda?" His voice rose with every word.

"I think you like it when I don't drink. I think you like feeling better than me. Like you're too good for what I need at the end of the day."

"Bob, please. The children—"

"The children need to see that their father isn't some kind of monster just because he wants a drink in his own house."

Then he picked up his dinner plate.

For a second, it looked normal in his hands. White ceramic with tiny blue flowers. Meatloaf, mashed potatoes, carrots. A normal plate, a normal dinner.

Then it hit the wall.

The crash shook the whole room. Pieces of ceramic flew across the table. Mashed potatoes and brown gravy slid down Mommy's family photos. One shard struck the window, leaving a cracked spider web that would stay there for years.

Leo started crying softly, trying to hide the sound. The kind of crying that came from deep in your chest but barely made it out, because noise could make everything worse.

"Bob, stop."

But Daddy was already moving. He reached for Mommy, his hand clamping around her wrist just above her wedding ring. I saw her face change from shock to pain.

"Don't you ever," he said, his voice low and hard, "tell me what I can and can't do in my own house."

Mommy's face went pale, but she didn't cry out. She never did. Then something shifted. Her eyes steadied.

"Let go of me, Bob," she said, quiet but firm. "You're hurting me. You're scaring your children."

"I'm not—"

"Look at them." She nodded toward us without breaking eye contact. "Look at what you're doing to them."

For a moment, his grip loosened. He turned his head, and I saw confusion flicker across his face, as if he wasn't sure how he'd ended up here.

"Bob," Mommy said, her voice calm, almost firm. "Let go of my arm and go sleep this off. We'll talk tomorrow."

It wasn't loud. It wasn't dramatic. But it was the first time I'd ever heard her tell him what to do instead of begging.

"Go to your room!" Daddy roared at us. "Both of you!"

We went. Not upstairs. Straight to the basement.

Leo crawled behind the big boxes of Christmas decorations, Rex pressed against his chest. I followed, dragging the dusty cardboard back in front of us until we were hidden.

The basement was cold, smelling of old concrete and mothballs, but it was safer than upstairs. We couldn't see Daddy's face anymore. Couldn't hear all the words, just the muffled roar of anger above our heads.

"Is M-Mommy gonna be okay?" Leo whispered.

"Mommy's tough," I whispered back, though my stomach hurt with doubt. "She can handle Daddy when he's like this."

"Why does he g-get like this?"

I didn't know how to explain it to him. That alcohol was poison. That it made Daddy sick and mean and lost, and that sometimes the person you loved could also be the person you feared.

"He just gets sick sometimes," I said. "Like when you get a cold, but different. It makes him angry instead of tired."

"Will he g-get better?"

I thought about my promise from Easter two years ago. The one carved deep into me like writing in wet cement.

"I don't know if Daddy will get better," I said finally. "But I know we'll be okay. You and me. We'll take care of each other."

Leo nodded and leaned against me, small and warm. Even at six, he understood. Sometimes, big sister was the only parent he had.

We stayed there until the yelling faded, until the house went quiet again.

When we crept upstairs, Mommy was in the kitchen sweeping up shards of the plate. There were red marks on her wrist where his hand had been, but she was humming softly as she worked, as if it was an ordinary night.

"There you are," she said when she spotted us. "Why don't you go brush your teeth? It's bedtime."

So we did. We brushed our teeth side by side, staring at our reflections in the mirror. Neither of us said a word about the crack in the window, the stains on the wall, or the bruises already rising on Mommy's arm.

In our family, silence was part of survival.

The next morning, the smell of bacon and pancakes pulled me awake.

Mickey Mouse pancakes.

I padded into the kitchen and found Daddy at the stove, humming while he flipped them. Round circles with blueberry eyes and bacon-strip smiles. He wore jeans and his Cleveland Indians shirt, his hair still damp from the shower. The light through the window made everything look bright, as if last night had never happened.

"Morning, princess!" he said, grinning wide. His voice was warm and cheerful. "Look what I'm making for my favorite kids."

This Daddy wasn't the one who threw a plate against the wall. This Daddy had soft eyes and steady hands and a smile that made me feel like the luckiest girl in Ohio.

"They look perfect, Daddy."

"Only the best for my princess. Now, go wake your brother. Tell him Mickey Mouse is waiting."

I turned to get Leo but stopped. Mommy was in the doorway, still in her robe. She was watching Daddy cook. Her face looked calm, but something in her eyes was different. Something that hadn't been there before last night.

"Bob," she said softly. "We need to talk."

"Sure, honey. After breakfast. Let's just have a nice morning first."

"No." Her voice was quiet but firm. "Now. Before the children come back."

Daddy's spatula froze in the air. "Linda, I don't think—"

"Last night was unacceptable." Her words came slow and even. "You broke a plate in front of our children. You grabbed me hard enough to leave bruises. That can't happen again."

"Honey, I was stressed from work—"

"I don't want excuses. I want to hear that you know it was wrong and that it won't happen again."

I stood in the hallway, not daring to move. This wasn't the Mommy who usually smoothed things over. This was someone I'd never seen before. Gentle still, but solid and unshaken.

"Of course it was wrong," Daddy said, his voice lower now. "I'm sorry, Linda. You know I'd never want to hurt you or scare the kids."

"Then you need help. Real help. Not just promises."

"I can control this—"

"No, Bob. You can't. And I won't let our children think this is normal."

They stared at each other across the little kitchen, the smell of bacon heavy in the air. I held my breath, waiting.

"We'll talk about it," Daddy said finally.

"Yes," Mommy answered, "we will."

It wasn't a big victory. No shouting, no slamming doors. But it was the first time I'd heard Mommy hold her ground.

I slipped away to get Leo. He was already awake, hiding under his covers with Rex. His eyes were wide.

"Is Daddy m-mad still?" he asked.

"No," I said. "He's making Mickey Mouse pancakes."

His face lit up but stayed puzzled. "The same Daddy from last night?"

That was the question that never left me. How could the man who threw plates and grabbed Mommy be the same man who hummed happy songs while he cooked pancakes with silly faces? How could both exist in one body?

"No," I said, because it was true even if it made no sense. "He is happy now."

At breakfast, Daddy cut Leo's pancakes into perfect bite-sized pieces. He made airplane noises to help him eat. He asked me about my reading level, pride shining in his face when I told him I was ahead. "That's my smart girl. I always knew you were special and smart."

No trace of last night in his voice. No hint of broken plates or bruises. It was as if the storm had never happened.

But I saw the faint purple marks on Mommy's wrist when she reached for the juice. I also noticed how Leo flinched each time Daddy moved too quickly, even if it was just to grab the syrup.

Our bodies remembered what the family was pretending to forget.

After breakfast, Daddy and Leo built a Lego tower together. He made sound effects for the crane and cheered when Leo figured out how to add wheels. They laughed side by side while I did my homework at the table.

Watching them, confusion pressed heavily in my chest. Both Daddies were real: the gentle one who played Legos and the dangerous one who made us run to the basement. I never knew which one would show up.

All I knew was that I had to pay attention. Watch, listen, be ready. Protect Leo from the version that wasn't safe.

That's how our basement refuge became real.

At first, it was only a hiding place. But I made it into more. I dragged down old pillows and blankets Mommy thought she'd lost. I found a working flashlight and stashed it behind the Christmas boxes. I even brought some of Leo's books and a deck of cards for the long nights.

"This is our safe place," I told him. "When it gets scary upstairs, we come here."

"Like a fort?" he asked.

"Exactly. Our secret fort."

Leo loved it. He named it Fort Rex after his dinosaur. He brought three more stuffed animals to guard the entrance. Within a week, he could find it in complete darkness without the flashlight.

I was proud of him. Proud he'd learned the game so well.

But sometimes, deep down, I wished we didn't have to play it so often.

School became my favorite place. Millfield Elementary was old and creaky, with books that smelled like dust and glue, but it felt safe. At school, adults spoke in calm voices. Nobody slammed doors or threw plates. The loudest noises were kids yelling on the playground or the squeaky wheels on Mr. Murphy's mop cart in the hallway.

Mrs. Morales, my third-grade teacher, started noticing things about me that first fall. How I jumped when a door banged shut. How my eyes kept drifting to the classroom doorway, as if I were waiting for someone scary to walk in. How I finished my lunch in three minutes, chewing so fast it made my stomach hurt, as if I thought someone might snatch it away.

"Olivia," she said one afternoon when I had finished my reading work half an hour before anyone else, "would you like to help me organize the library tomorrow during lunch? I could use someone who loves books as much as you do."

I nodded right away. Mrs. Morales's classroom was always quiet, always steady. And I did love books. More than sitting in the noisy cafeteria where kids asked why I ate so fast.

"Yes, I'd love to," I said, and I meant it more than she probably knew.

Her classroom became my hiding place. Every lunch period, I sorted books, wiped the whiteboard, and sharpened pencils. She asked gentle questions about my family, and I gave her careful answers that weren't lies but weren't the whole truth either. She never pushed. She just gave me space where I could breathe normally for forty-five minutes.

Leo was learning his own ways to cope.

His stutter grew worse as the leaves turned brown and the days got colder, especially after nights when Daddy had been drinking. But he discovered something else. He could make people laugh. Real laughter. Not polite smiles.

"Why d-did the chicken cross the playground?" he asked one night at dinner. Daddy had already had three beers but was still smiling, still himself.

"I don't know, buddy. Why?"

"To get to the other slide!"

Daddy roared with laughter, loud and genuine. "That's a good one! Where'd you hear that?"

"M-my friend told me at school."

"That's hilarious! Linda, did you hear that? Our boy's a comedian!"

The whole room shifted. Just like that, the tension melted. Daddy leaned back in his chair, grinning, and Leo grinned too, soaking it up.

For the rest of dinner, Leo kept telling jokes. Some were funny, some made no sense at all, but his timing was perfect.

He had figured out how to fill a room with laughter, how to push fear into the corner by making people smile.

I was proud of him.

I was also sad he had to learn that skill at such a young age.

Two weeks after the plate-shattering night, something unexpected happened. Daddy had been sober for five days—long enough that Mommy's bruises had faded from dark purple to yellow.

That's when he knocked on my bedroom door.

"Princess? Can I come in?"

I looked up from my homework, my stomach tightening as I studied his face. I had learned to check for danger before he even spoke. But this was normal Daddy. His eyes were clear, his hands steady, his voice soft in a way that made me feel safe.

"Sure, Daddy."

He sat on the edge of my bed, holding a small wooden box I had never seen before.

"I want to show you something," he said. "Something that belonged to my daddy when I was your age."

He opened it carefully, as if it were fragile. Inside was a compass, real brass, resting on faded blue velvet. Not the cheap plastic kind from school, but heavy, polished, with tiny numbers around the edges and a needle that kept pointing north no matter how I turned it.

"This was your grandpa's," Daddy said. "He gave it to me when I turned eight. And now I want you to have it."

I didn't know much about Grandpa. Only that he died when Daddy was sixteen and that they'd "had their troubles." But watching how gently Daddy held the compass, I knew this mattered.

"See this needle?" He pointed at the slim red arrow. "No matter how lost you are, it always points north. Always shows you the way home."

Then he looked at me. His blue eyes, just like mine, filled with something I almost never saw there: hope.

"I'm giving it to you because you're my compass, Olivia. You always know what's right. You take care of Leo, you help your mommy, you work hard in school. Even when things get crazy, you stay pointed in the right direction."

He placed it in my hands. It felt heavy, warmer than I expected from his touch. The needle swung, then settled back north.

"I was young when I started drinking," he said quietly. "I thought it would help with the pain of losing my daddy. But do you know what happened instead?"

I shook my head, too afraid to break the fragile honesty in his voice.

"I lost my compass," he said. "I started making choices that pulled me away from everything good. Away from being the man my daddy wanted me to be."

He touched my cheek, steady and warm.

"But you, princess, you've got a compass inside you that nothing can break. I can see it. The way you protect Leo, the way you stay strong. Promise me you'll never lose that. Promise me you'll trust yourself."

"I promise, Daddy."

"Good girl. My good, good girl."

He kissed my forehead, and for ten minutes we sat there together, talking about Grandpa's Navy stories and sailors following the stars. For ten minutes, I had the Daddy I dreamed of: patient, gentle, fully present.

Then he went back to his room, and soon I heard the crack of a beer can opening.

I kept the compass on my nightstand. Every night before bed, I held it and watched the arrow swing north. It became my treasure, proof that inside the man who scared me was still a father who loved me enough to give me his most precious memory.

But the compass made things more confusing. Because how do you hold both truths in your hands?

A father who gives you a family heirloom, and the same father who makes you hide in the basement?

How do you love someone who sees your goodness but can't find his own?

At eight years old, I didn't understand that addiction could make someone both tender and destructive. That the man who wanted to guide me home could be completely lost himself.

Three days later, I came home from school and found Daddy in the kitchen, gripping an empty Jack Daniel's bottle as if it were proof of some terrible crime.

"LINDA!" he roared, his voice booming so loudly the windows rattled. "LINDA, GET DOWN HERE RIGHT NOW!"

I didn't wait. I grabbed Leo's hand and pulled him toward the basement stairs before Mommy even answered. Behind us, Daddy's rage built louder and louder, like thunder rolling closer. I knew this one was going to be bad.

Worse than plates smashing against the wall. Worse than Mommy's wrists turning purple.

In our hiding spot behind the Christmas boxes, we curled together and listened. Daddy's voice filled the house, shouting Mommy's name again and again, each one louder, sharper, scarier.

I wrapped my arms around Leo, pressing his head to my chest. "I will never be like him," I whispered into his hair. "Never, never, never."

Leo nodded against me, his little body warm, his heart pounding so hard I could feel it through his ribs. Rex, his green dinosaur, was squished tight between us. I rubbed the stuffed fabric with my thumb, the soft fuzz familiar against my skin while the house shook with Daddy's rage.

Another crash came from upstairs. Not just a plate this time. Something bigger. Maybe a chair. Maybe the lamp in the living room.

"LINDA!" Daddy roared again, his voice shaking the air all the way down to the basement walls.

Leo burrowed deeper into my shoulder.

"It's okay," I whispered, even though it wasn't. "He'll get tired soon. He always does."

And he would. After another hour, maybe two, the shouting would turn to silence. The crashes would stop. Then we'd hear the heavy footsteps, the creak of the recliner, and finally nothing. That's when Mommy would find us, her face calm and collected as if she hadn't just lived through three hours of hell. And we'd all pretend it hadn't happened.

I reached into my pocket and pulled out Grandpa's compass. The brass felt cold and solid. I flipped it open with my thumb. The red needle swung, then steadied.

Leo lifted his head just enough to look. His eyes were huge in the half-dark, shining with fear but also trust.

I held it between us so he could see. He reached out and touched the glass face with one finger, gentle, as if it might break.

I snapped it shut and kept it tight in my palm.

Then the yelling stopped.

We sat frozen in the quiet, waiting. The heavy footsteps came next, uneven and slow, moving into the living room. The familiar squeak of the recliner springs followed.

"Is it over?" Leo whispered.

"For tonight," I said.

I kept holding him, my cheek pressed to his hair, the compass warm now in my hand. I wasn't ready to move yet. Down here in the basement, with Leo breathing against me, I could almost pretend tomorrow was a normal school day. That Mrs. Morales would ask me about my weekend. That I had spelling tests and math problems waiting.

"Come on," I said at last, helping Leo stand. "Let's go see if Mommy's okay."

I slid the compass back into my pocket and made sure it was secure before we climbed the stairs.

Chapter Three

The Little Thief

*W*INTER 2002

The Christmas grocery money disappeared on a Wednesday.

I knew because I'd been watching Mommy count the envelope every night at the kitchen table, her lips moving silently as she added up the bills. She'd spread the twenties out like they were fragile treasures. Enough for ham, potatoes, maybe even the ingredients for her sugar cookies. The ones that made Leo's whole face light up.

"Forty, sixty, eighty, one hundred," she'd whisper. "One twenty, one forty."

One hundred and forty dollars. Enough to make us feel like other families for one day. Enough to pretend Daddy's drinking hadn't stolen Christmas too.

But Wednesday morning, the envelope was empty.

I walked into the kitchen at six in the morning and found Mommy still in her waitress uniform from the night before, hunched over the table. She was staring at a torn envelope as if sheer focus might make it whole again. Behind her, Daddy snored in their bedroom, that harsh rattling snore that only came when he'd passed out drunk.

"Mommy?" I whispered. "What's wrong?"

She looked up. Her eyes were dry now, like she'd already cried everything out.

"The Christmas money's gone, baby."

"Gone where?"

But I already knew. We both knew. Daddy had lost his job Friday, and he'd been on a five-day binge since. Beer bottles and whiskey. Anything to help him forget.

"Did Daddy take it?"

Her face crumpled. For a second, she looked younger than thirty-one. She looked like someone's daughter, not my mother, not the woman trying to figure out how to explain that Santa wasn't coming this year.

"I don't know," she said. "It was just... gone."

But I'd seen the bottles piled in the trash. At least fifteen empty beer cans. Three empty whiskey bottles. More than a hundred and forty dollars' worth of poison.

Daddy had drunk our Christmas.

"What are we going to do?" I asked.

"I don't know, sweetheart. I don't know."

That was Wednesday. By Friday, Christmas Eve, we'd been eating saltines and tap water for three days.

It wasn't that there was no other food. There was a can of green beans, half a loaf of stale bread, a box of instant oatmeal gone soft with humidity. Mommy was saving them for "emergencies." I didn't understand why crackers for three days didn't count as an emergency.

Leo had stopped saying he was hungry by Thursday. He figured out quickly that complaining only made Mommy cry. So instead, he played games with the crackers.

"Pretend they're fancy cookies," he told me Friday morning, holding up a saltine like it was made of gold. "Pretend we're rich kids having a tea party."

"What kind of cookies?" I asked, playing along because it was better than discussing the ache in our stomachs.

"The kind that cost... a million dollars each. And we're so rich we eat them for breakfast every day."

He even fed pretend cookies to Rex, pressing crackers to the stuffed dinosaur's mouth and making chewing sounds.

That Friday afternoon, I made my decision. I was going to fix this.

Leo napped on the couch with Rex under his arm while Mommy lay in her room, staring at the ceiling. She'd called in sick, saying she couldn't face waiting tables on Christmas Eve.

"Mommy, I'm going to walk to Kroger," I told her.

She sat up quickly. "What? Why?"

"To look at the decorations. Leo wants to see the big tree in front of the store."

It wasn't a total lie. Leo did love that giant fake tree with red and gold ornaments. But that wasn't why I was going.

"Olivia, I don't have money for anything at Kroger."

"I know. We're just looking."

She studied me closely, like she was trying to see through my face. I kept mine as plain as I could, like I was just a kid wanting to see pretty lights, not a thief planning her first crime.

"Take Leo with you," she said finally. "Stay together. Don't talk to strangers. Come straight home."

"I will."

Leo perked up when I told him. He zipped his winter coat and carefully arranged Rex in his backpack so the dinosaur could see.

"Are we just looking at d-decorations?" he asked, his breath puffing white in the cold air as we walked toward the plaza.

"Yeah," I lied. "Just looking."

Kroger was packed. Shoppers pushed carts filled with hams, turkeys, potatoes, and pies. I watched a woman in a red coat load her cart with sweet potatoes, whipped cream, and cranberry sauce. Enough food for a feast.

"Look at all the food," Leo whispered, eyes wide.

"I know."

"Do you think Santa shops here too?"

"Maybe," I said, though I'd stopped believing two years earlier. Real Santa wouldn't give rich kids more than poor kids.

We walked slowly, Leo pointing out decorations while I kept a mental list of what we needed: ham, rolls, potatoes, green beans, cookies if I was lucky.

The plan was simple. Wait until Leo was distracted, slip the food into my backpack, and walk out. I'd seen kids steal candy before. No one would suspect a nine-year-old.

My chance came in the bakery. Leo pressed his nose to the glass case, staring at frosted cookies shaped like Santas and trees.

"They look like Mommy's," he said.

"They do."

While he stared, I moved quickly. Two packs of dinner rolls. A small ham, the cheapest one I could find. A bag of potatoes. A can of green beans. My heart pounded so loudly I thought someone would hear it. But nobody looked at me. We were just kids admiring Christmas cookies.

"Olivia, look at this one!" Leo called, pointing at a Santa cookie. "It looks just like the real Santa!"

"It does," I said, slipping a box of chocolate chip cookies into my bag. Leo deserved something sweet on Christmas morning, even if it was stolen.

"Can we get some cookies?" he asked hopefully.

"Not today, Leo. Remember, we're just looking."

He nodded, disappointed, and moved on to the cakes. I followed, my backpack heavy with stolen food.

We were steps from the exit when I felt a hand close on my shoulder.

"Excuse me, young lady."

I turned, my heart sinking. A man in a Kroger vest stood over me, his eyes sharp and suspicious. His name tag said *Mr. Peterson.* I knew him. The manager. The one I'd seen scolding cashiers and arguing with customers about coupons.

"Open your backpack," he said.

My stomach dropped to my shoes. I tried to look confused instead of terrified. "What?"

"Your backpack. Let me see what's inside."

Leo's small voice rose beside me. "What's happening?" His blue eyes were wide and already wet.

"Nothing," I said quickly. "Just a misunderstanding."

But it wasn't. We all knew it. Mr. Peterson had been watching me, waiting. He'd seen everything.

"The backpack," he repeated, louder now, his voice carrying across the busy store. Shoppers turned to look.

My hands trembled as I unzipped it.

He reached inside and pulled out the ham first, holding it high like proof. Then the rolls. The potatoes. The cookies. Piece after piece, everything I had taken to try to save Christmas.

"Well, well, well," he said, his lip curling. "Looks like we've got ourselves a little criminal."

The word hit me like a slap. Criminal. Was that who I was? I wasn't trying to be bad. I was trying to help. But the way he stared at me made me feel like dirt.

"I'm sorry," I whispered. "I didn't mean—"

"You didn't mean to steal fifty dollars' worth of groceries?" he snapped. "You didn't mean to walk out without paying?"

Fifty dollars. More than a third of the money Daddy had drunk away. More than I'd ever held in my hands.

"My family—" I started, my voice breaking.

"I don't want excuses," he cut me off. "Stealing is stealing."

A group of people gathered to look at us. They had shopping carts full of food and nice winter coats, and they stared at me and Leo like we were something strange. I heard them talking to each other in mean whispers: *What's wrong with those parents? That kid has no manners.*

I didn't understand why they were being so mean. I was just trying to help.

"I should call the police," Mr. Peterson said loudly so everyone could hear. "That's what happens to kids who steal."

Leo started crying so hard his whole body was shaking. I wanted to hug him, but I was too scared to move. The shame felt like having a really bad fever, burning up but also freezing. My stomach hurt, my face felt hot, and I couldn't breathe right. All the people staring at us made me want to hide under a rock.

"Please don't call the police," I said, but my voice came out all squeaky. "I'll never do it again, I promise."

"You won't get the chance," he said, looking pleased about being cruel to me. "You can't ever come in this store again. And if I see you stealing anywhere else, I'll tell everyone what you really are."

I was crying so hard I could barely see anything. Everything looked blurry and watery.

"A THIEF!" he yelled. "A LITTLE CRIMINAL!"

Those words felt like getting punched in the stomach. *Little criminal.* Was I really bad now? I thought about the promise I made to God on the bathroom floor, about how I said I'd always be good. I thought about the dead rabbit in our backyard and how I told it I'd be different when I grew up. But now this man was calling me a criminal in front of all these people, and maybe he was right. Maybe good kids don't steal food, even when their families are hungry.

I didn't feel like a criminal. I felt like a little girl who just wanted her brother to have something to eat on Christmas. But all these grown-ups were looking at me like I was something scary and bad.

I wanted to tell them we were hungry. I wanted to explain that Mommy was working so hard her feet hurt and we didn't have money for food. I wanted to tell them Leo was pretending crackers were cookies because he didn't understand why we had to be so hungry all the time. But I couldn't make any words come out. I just stood there crying while Leo cried too, and all these people stared at us.

"For God's sake, she's just a child, and it's Christmas."

A kind voice came from behind all the mean people. I looked up and saw Mrs. Campbell. She was one of the nice ladies who worked at the store. Sometimes when Mommy brought me here, she would smile at me and ask how school was going.

She had gray hair like a grandma and kind eyes. When she looked at me, she didn't seem scared or mad. She looked sad, like when you see a hurt puppy.

"She should know better," Mr. Peterson said, still being mean.

"She's hungry," Mrs. Campbell said. Her voice was quiet, but it made Mr. Peterson stop talking. "And she loves her family."

She was right. I did love my family. That's why I took the food. Not because I was bad, but because I loved them.

"That doesn't make stealing okay—"

"How much does it cost?" Mrs. Campbell asked.

"Fifty-three dollars and forty-seven cents," he said.

Mrs. Campbell opened her purse. It was old and soft-looking, like my mommy's but nicer. She took out some twenty-dollar bills and handed them to Mr. Peterson.

"There. Now it's paid for."

Mr. Peterson's mouth opened like a fish. "You're paying for the stuff she stole?"

"I'm paying for Christmas dinner," she said. "For a family that needs it."

She came over and knelt down so she was the same height as me. Her eyes were so nice they made me cry even more, but it was different crying. Like when you're hurt, but someone gives you a hug.

"Every little girl deserves Christmas dinner," she said. "Take the food home, sweetie."

Then she opened her purse again and gave me a twenty-dollar bill. It felt warm and smelled like peppermints.

"Give this to your mommy," she whispered. "Tell her Santa wanted to help."

I could barely talk because I was crying so much, but I managed to say, "Thank you."

She was like an angel, but a real one who worked at the grocery store and had gray hair.

"Go home now," she said, soft and kind. "Merry Christmas."

Leo and I left the store in silence. My backpack felt heavier now, not just with food but with shame and relief tangled together.

Leo sniffled. "Are you in trouble, Livvy?"

"I don't know."

"Are you a criminal?"

The question twisted my stomach. That man had called me a thief in front of everyone. And I had stolen. But I wasn't trying to hurt anyone; I was trying to save us.

"I don't think so," I said finally. "I think I was just trying to help."

"Like a hero?"

Heroes in movies always saved people, and everyone cheered. Nobody cheered for me. Heroes didn't steal ham in grocery stores.

"Maybe," I said. "But heroes probably don't steal."

"Even if it's to save Christmas?"

"I don't know, Leo. I really don't know."

We took the long way home, through the rich side of town where the houses were twice the size of ours. Warm yellow light spilled from every window. Through the glass, I saw glowing trees, piles of presents, families laughing around tables.

I felt like I was staring into another world.

One house made me stop walking.

It was enormous, with tall white pillars like something out of a movie. Through the giant front window, I saw a family gathered around their Christmas tree. The parents were young and laughing, their faces glowing in the soft light. Two kids about Leo's age and mine tore into shiny boxes that looked like early presents. The tree itself was huge, covered in lights and ornaments, topped with a star that probably cost more than Mommy's entire Christmas budget had ever been.

I stood on the sidewalk, staring as if I were watching creatures from another planet. How did families like that exist? How could some kids sit around giant trees opening gifts while other kids had to steal ham just to have dinner?

"They look happy," Leo whispered.

"Yeah," I said. "They do."

"Do you think they ever get hungry?"

"No," I told him. "I don't think they do."

That's when I caught my reflection in their window: a nine-year-old girl with tangled hair, a streaked face, a coat too small, and boots that pinched. I looked exactly like what Mr. Peterson had called me: a little criminal. Someone who didn't belong in a neighborhood like this, peeking through windows at other people's joy.

And right then, staring at that family, I made another promise to myself. A big one. Like the promise I'd made on the bathroom floor when I was six.

Someday my kids would never have to steal food. My kids would sit around Christmas trees with full bellies and piles of presents. I'd have enough money to keep them safe from everything.

"Come on," I said, tugging Leo away. "Let's go home."

Christmas dinner that night was strange, wonderful, and heavy all at once.

Mommy cried when Leo and I walked in with the backpack full of food. She hugged me so tightly I couldn't breathe, whispering, "I'm sorry" into my hair over and over, as if she were the one who'd done something wrong.

"You should never have had to do that," she said. "Children shouldn't have to take care of their families."

But I had done it. And it had worked. We had ham and potatoes and rolls for Christmas. Even if it came with shame and a lifetime ban from Kroger, it worked.

Mommy cooked the ham while Leo and I sat at the table, eating for the first time in days. The food was hot, salty, and heavy in my stomach, the best thing I'd ever tasted.

"This is the best dinner ever," Leo said, his cheeks full of bread.

"It is," I agreed. But every bite burned a little with shame.

Around seven o'clock, Daddy stumbled out of the bedroom, bleary and unsteady, still smelling like the bender he'd been sleeping off. He stared at the table, at the steaming food, his face confused.

"Where did all this come from?" he asked.

"Olivia got it," Leo said proudly.

Daddy turned to me, his eyes bloodshot. "How'd you get it, princess?"

I looked at Mommy. She gave the tiniest shake of her head. We weren't going to tell him. Not about the stealing. Not about Mrs. Campbell's kindness. Not about how close we'd come to losing Christmas completely.

"A nice lady at the store helped us," I said instead.

"That's... that's good," he said slowly. He sat at the table, staring at the ham like he couldn't believe it was real. "That's really good."

He tried to eat with us, but his hands shook and his stomach turned against him. After a few bites, he lowered his head to the table and passed out with his face in the mashed potatoes.

Leo and I kept eating while Daddy snored into his plate.

"Is Daddy okay?" Leo whispered.

"He's just tired," I said, the lie coming quickly now, easily.

"Will he be better tomorrow? For Christmas?"

I looked at Daddy's face. His skin was pale, tinged with yellow. His breathing was shallow and rattly. Drool slid from his mouth into the food Mommy had cooked from the groceries I stole.

"I hope so, Leo."

But I didn't believe it. Deep down, I was beginning to understand that Daddy's sickness wasn't the kind that rest or medicine could fix. It was the kind that grew worse until it either killed you or left you wishing it had.

After dinner, while Mommy washed dishes and Daddy slept on at the table, Leo and I sat on the couch in front of our little tree. It held twelve ornaments we'd made from paper and popsicle sticks. No presents sat beneath it. Rent and heat had taken what little money there was.

Still, our bellies were full for the first time in three days, and that felt like its own gift.

"Livvy?" Leo asked quietly, curled up beside me with Rex in his lap.

"Yeah?"

"Will we always be hungry?"

The question hit me like a blow because I didn't know the answer.

Would we always be hungry? Would we always be the family that ate crackers for three days, depending on a nine-year-old to steal Christmas dinner? Would Leo grow up thinking hunger was normal, that shame was part of survival, that love meant watching the people who were supposed to protect you destroy themselves with poison?

"I don't know," I told him because he deserved the truth, even when it hurt.

Leo nodded like he'd expected that answer all along.

"But I promise you something," I said, thinking about the rich family in the window and the vow I'd made on the sidewalk. "When I grow up, when I have my own kids, they'll never be hungry. Never. I'll make sure they always have enough food, enough money, enough of everything so they never feel like this."

"How will you do that?"

"I'll be rich. Really rich. Rich enough that nobody can ever make my kids feel the way we felt today."

"Rich like the people in the big houses?"

"Richer," I said. "Rich enough to buy Christmas dinner without even thinking about it. Rich enough to buy all the food at Kroger."

Leo smiled then, the first real smile I'd seen in days. "That sounds nice."

"It will be nice," I said. "It will be perfect."

And I meant every word.

From the kitchen came a loud crash, followed by Daddy's muffled swearing. Probably the chair tipping over when he tried to sit again. But I didn't move to check, didn't scramble to clean up his mess like I usually did. Tonight, I just pulled Leo closer and let Daddy take care of himself.

"Tell me about the rich house again," Leo whispered.

"It'll have a big kitchen with a refrigerator that's always full," I said softly. "And a Christmas tree so tall it touches the ceiling, covered in lights you can see from space."

"And presents?"

"Mountains of presents. So many that we'd open them all day long."

Leo giggled, that sweet sound I hadn't heard in three days. "That's too many presents."

"There's no such thing," I told him.

Outside, snow had started to fall. Big, soft flakes drifted down, making the old apartment building look almost clean, almost magical. Christmas Eve snow. The kind people said could make everything new.

I pressed my forehead against the cold window and thought about the twenty-dollar bill Mrs. Campbell had slipped me, still crumpled in my coat pocket. Tomorrow, Mommy could buy pancake mix and maybe some juice, and it would feel like a feast compared to the crackers we'd been living on.

But someday, someday soon, I wouldn't need kind strangers to save Christmas for us.

"Livvy?" Leo's voice was heavy with sleep.

"Yeah?"

"Are you really gonna be rich?"

I looked at his small face, tired but hopeful, still trusting after everything. Even after being caught stealing. Even after walking through neighborhoods lit up with everything we didn't have.

"Yeah," I said, and I felt the promise sink into me, the way my bathroom floor vow had three years earlier. "I'm really gonna be rich."

Leo's breathing slowed, deep and steady, until I knew he was asleep. But I stayed awake. I watched the snow fall, listened to Daddy's rough snores from the kitchen, and pulled Grandpa's compass from my pocket.

I opened it carefully so it wouldn't click too loudly. In the dim streetlight outside, the needle still pointed north, steady and true.

Tomorrow was Christmas. We'd eat pancakes. Leo would play with Rex. Maybe Daddy would even stay sober long enough to help us clean the kitchen.

But tonight, with Leo asleep against me and snow falling softly outside, I made plans.

Plans for studying hard. Plans for jobs that paid enough to buy Christmas dinner without stealing. Plans for a life where my children would never be hungry and never be called a thief.

I watched the compass needle point north, steady as ever, and I let my eyes follow it until I finally fell asleep too.

Chapter Four

There's No Place Like Home (When Home Is Hell)

S*PRING 2003*

"Olivia Parker, you will play Dorothy."

Mrs. Henderson's voice rang out in the multipurpose room, and for a second, I couldn't breathe. Thirty of us stood in a line, waiting for her to read the cast list for *The Wizard of Oz*. And she'd just said my name.

Dorothy. The lead. The part every single girl wanted.

Me.

"Congratulations, sweetheart," Mrs. Henderson said, peering at me over her wire-rimmed glasses, her eyes kind and twinkly.

"You have a beautiful voice and perfect stage presence. Dorothy has to be brave and determined, someone the audience believes in. That's you."

I floated home from school that day, as if my shoes weren't even touching the ground. For once, maybe for the first time in my ten years, I had something that was mine. Something that wasn't about Daddy's drinking or Mommy's worry or Leo's stuttering. Something untouched by the chaos of our house.

This was proof I was good at something. Proof I wasn't just Bob Parker's daughter.

I was Dorothy. I was the star.

"Guess what!" I shouted as I pushed open our front door, my chest buzzing with excitement.

Mommy looked up from folding laundry at the kitchen table. The warm smell of detergent filled the air. Leo sat on the floor surrounded by Legos, Rex propped against a tower like he was guarding it.

"What is it, baby?"

"I got Dorothy! In the school play! I'm the star!"

Mommy's face lit up with real joy, not the thin smile she wore most of the time. She dropped the towel and pulled me into her arms. She smelled like clean laundry and the vanilla lotion she wore when she wanted to feel pretty.

"Oh, Olivia! That's wonderful. I'm so proud of you!"

"What's Dorothy?" Leo asked, tilting his head.

"She's the main character," I explained quickly. "She gets to wear ruby slippers and sing *Somewhere Over the Rainbow*, and she's the most important person in the whole show."

"Cool! Will you sing it for us?"

I was just about to start when Daddy walked in from the living room with a beer in his hand. It was only four-thirty, but I already knew it wasn't his first bottle from the way he looked.

"What's all the excitement?" he asked, sitting down slowly and carefully, like someone trying to hide how unsteady they were.

"Olivia got the lead in the play," Mommy said. Her voice was bright, but I could hear the edge beneath it. She'd heard the slur in his words too.

For just a moment, Daddy's whole face changed. His eyes cleared. The proud father peeked through the fog. I saw the man who had once given me Grandpa's compass and told me I was his guiding star.

"Dorothy? You got Dorothy?" He set down the beer, his eyes locking onto mine. "That's incredible, princess. That's... God, that's amazing."

"The show's in three weeks," I said quickly. "On a Friday night. Mrs. Henderson says the whole town comes."

"Of course they do. And they'll see my daughter up there, brilliant and perfect." He reached out and touched my cheek. His hand was warm and steady. "I'm proud of you, Olivia. So proud."

For that moment, I felt like the luckiest girl in Ohio. Not just because of the part, but because Daddy was proud of me. For once, I didn't have to feel ashamed of being his daughter. I imagined people in the audience pointing at me and saying, *That Bob Parker must be doing something right to have a daughter like that.*

"You'll come, right?" I asked, suddenly anxious. "You'll watch me be Dorothy?"

"Wouldn't miss it for the world, princess. Not for anything."

The next three weeks blurred into rehearsals and practice.

I drilled my lines until I could say them backward in my sleep. I sang my songs in the shower, on the way to school, and under my breath while brushing my teeth. I memorized everyone else's parts too, just in case.

"Olivia, you know this play better than I do," Mrs. Henderson laughed one afternoon after I corrected another student's blocking. "You could direct it yourself."

But it wasn't about directing. It was about being perfect. Flawless.

Because if I was perfect enough on that stage, if I shone bright enough, maybe people would see me and not the family I came from. They'd forget about the drunk man who had been carried out of the school fundraiser by two other dads. Maybe they'd see me instead of him.

At home, I practiced in front of my mirror, watching every expression until it looked just right. Leo was my most loyal fan, sitting cross-legged on my bed with Rex in his lap, clapping after every song.

"You're r-really good, Livvy," he told me one night after I'd run through the whole play for him. "Better than the people on TV."

"Thanks, Leo. You're going to love it. It's going to be amazing."

"Will Daddy really come?" he asked quietly.

The question made me freeze.

Leo had learned, just like I had, not to trust Daddy's promises. We both knew there was a world of difference between *wouldn't miss it for the world* and actually showing up when the night came, especially when there was alcohol involved.

"He promised," I told Leo, but the words felt shaky in my mouth. That knot of fear tightened in my stomach the way it always did when Daddy made big promises.

"But what if he d-doesn't?" Leo asked softly. "What if he gets sick, like for the Christmas concert last year?"

I remembered too. Him in second grade, one of twenty little kids singing carols onstage. Daddy had promised to come then too. We'd found him passed out in the garage instead, the car running, keys still in his hand, like he'd tried but couldn't make it.

"This is different," I said firmly. "This isn't just some little concert. This is the lead role. The biggest play of the year. Daddy won't miss it."

I had to believe that. I needed to. Because the picture of myself standing under those bright lights, singing my heart out to an empty seat where he should be. That was too painful to even think about.

The week of the play, I hardly slept. I went over my lines again and again, mouthing them in the dark, whispering them under my breath while walking to school. My Dorothy costume hung on my closet door like a promise: blue gingham dress, puffy sleeves, shiny red shoes smothered in glitter.

When I put it on for the final rehearsal, I looked in the mirror and felt a jolt of wonder. I didn't look like Olivia Parker, daughter of a drunk. I looked like someone from a movie. Someone important who belonged on a stage.

"You look beautiful, sweetheart," Mommy said, tying the bow in my hair. Her hands smelled like lotion and detergent.

"I feel like Dorothy," I said. And I did. I felt like if I clicked my heels, I could fly somewhere far away. Somewhere over the rainbow. Somewhere safer.

The night of the performance, I woke from a nightmare where I forgot every line and stood frozen while the whole crowd laughed at me. My sheets were damp with sweat, and even though it was still dark outside, I couldn't fall back asleep. I just lay there whispering my songs until the sun came up.

At breakfast, Daddy was drinking coffee instead of beer. That alone felt like a miracle.

"Big day, princess," he said, ruffling my hair. His hand was warm and steady. "You ready to show this town how talented you are?"

"I think so," I said. "I know all my lines."

"Of course you do. You're a Parker. Parkers don't do things halfway." He winked, and I felt that swell of pride and love I always felt when he was sober and present. This was the daddy I wanted in the front row.

"You'll be there early, right? Seven-thirty sharp. Mrs. Henderson said it starts on time."

"I'll be there at seven-fifteen," he said. "Front row center, cheering for my star."

All day at school, I buzzed with nerves. Teachers wished me luck. Kids I didn't even know well stopped me in the hall to say they couldn't wait to see it. Even the lunch ladies gave me an extra cookie and told me to break a leg.

By the time I got home, my body felt like it was buzzing out of my skin.

"Olivia, slow down," Mommy said, watching me pace circles around the living room. "You're going to wear yourself out before you even step on stage."

"I can't help it," I said. "What if I mess up? What if I forget my lines? What if my voice cracks on *Over the Rainbow*?"

"Sweetheart, you've sung that song a hundred times. You could do it in your sleep."

"But what if—"

"Olivia." Daddy's voice came from the kitchen, firm but gentle. "Come here."

I walked in and found him at the table, hands wrapped around a coffee mug. His eyes were clear. His movements were steady. Sober Daddy.

"Sit down, princess."

I sat across from him, my stomach churning with nerves.

"You know what I see when I look at you?" he asked.

I shook my head.

"I see a girl who's been brave since she was six years old, who takes care of everyone, works harder than anyone else, and never gives up." He leaned forward, reaching for my hand. His palm was warm against mine. "You think I don't notice how you look after Leo when I'm... when I'm not doing so well. You think I don't see how smart you are, how kind you are to your mother, how sometimes you hold this family together."

My throat closed. Daddy didn't usually talk this way. Not this plainly. Not about the truth we all knew but never said.

"Tonight, you get to show everybody else what I already know," he went on. "That Olivia Parker is extraordinary. That she's going to do amazing things with her life."

"What if I mess up?" I whispered.

"Then you'll keep going," he said. "But you won't mess up because you don't know how to do things halfway." His voice grew thick. "And I'll be so proud watching you, prouder than I've ever been in my life."

"Promise you'll be there?" I asked, needing it one more time. "Promise you'll come straight from work? On time?"

Something flickered in his eyes: guilt, shame, maybe a memory of all the times he hadn't kept his word. But he didn't look away.

"I promise, Olivia," he said. "Front row center, at seven-fifteen sharp. You have my word."

I believed him. Sitting in the kitchen with his steady hands wrapped around mine, his clear eyes shining with love, I believed him. I believed this time would be different. This time he wouldn't let me down.

By six o'clock, I was at school in the multipurpose room that had turned into backstage. Kids in costumes ran everywhere, their shoes squeaking on the linoleum. Parents hovered with powder and lipstick. Teachers shouted over the noise, trying to keep the chaos from spiraling out of control.

I sat in front of a tiny mirror while Mrs. Patterson dabbed blush onto my cheeks. Her hand smelled like soap and perfume.

"There you go, Dorothy," she said with a smile. "Perfect."

I leaned toward the glass. My blue eyes looked wide and shiny, almost too big for my face. My hair was curled into ringlets with blue ribbons that matched my dress. The gingham was crisp, and the sleeves puffed just right. For the first time in my life, I didn't look like Bob Parker's daughter. I looked like Dorothy. I looked like a star.

"Places in fifteen!" Mrs. Henderson called. "Dorothy, how are you feeling?"

"Perfect," I said, and I meant it. My nerves had hardened into focus. I was ready. Every crisis at home, every night I'd protected Leo, every moment I'd held myself together. It all led to this.

Tonight, I was going to prove I was more than my father's shadow.

At seven-twenty, I peeked through the curtain. The room was full. Every seat was occupied. Parents. Grandparents. Kids with siblings on stage. My eyes found them in the third row: Mommy in her best dress, Leo clutching Rex so tightly his little fingers looked white. But the seat beside Mommy was empty.

Seven-twenty-five. Still empty.

Seven-twenty-eight. My chest pounded. Maybe traffic. Maybe work.

"Places, everyone!"

The lights dimmed. The curtain rose. And when the audience saw me standing there as Dorothy, I felt like the most important person in the whole world.

I knew every single word. I hit every note perfectly. When I walked across the stage, my ruby slippers sparkled under the lights, and my blue dress swished just right. I could see people in the audience smiling at me, and some were even crying during the sad parts.

When I got to sing the rainbow song, the whole room got so quiet you could hear a pin drop. I sang it like I meant every word, like I really was Dorothy wanting to fly away to somewhere better. When I finished, everyone started clapping so loudly it made my ears ring. Some people even stood up! I felt like I was glowing, like I was made of sunshine.

This was the best night of my whole life. I was doing it! I was perfect!

And then I heard Daddy's voice.

"THAT'S MY DAUGHTER! THAT'S MY LITTLE GIRL UP THERE!"

For just one second, my heart jumped up to the sky. Daddy came! He was here to see me be Dorothy! He was proud of me!

But then I heard other sounds. People going "shhh" really loudly. Chairs scraping. Whispers everywhere.

"SHE'S BRILLIANT! THAT'S MY OLIVIA! I TAUGHT HER TO SING, YOU KNOW!"

Oh no, oh no, oh no.

Through the bright lights, I could see him walking down the aisle between all the seats. He was wobbling like he might fall over. He had a big bottle in his hand. And he was loud. Too loud. The bad kind of loud that meant he'd been drinking the scary drinks.

"Sir, please," I heard Mrs. Henderson say from somewhere in the dark. "Sir, you need to—"

"I'M JUST SO PROUD! LOOK AT HER! LOOK HOW TALENTED SHE IS!"

Now everyone was looking back and forth between me on the stage and Daddy stumbling around with his bottle.

I heard them whispering things like, "Is that her dad?" and "He's so drunk" and "That poor little girl."

My face got hot, and my stomach felt sick. I tried to keep saying my lines like nothing was wrong, but my brain felt all fuzzy. The boy playing the Scarecrow was looking at me with big, scared eyes, waiting for me to say my next words, but I couldn't remember what they were.

Daddy got all the way to the front and stood right in front of the stage. He was swaying back and forth and grinning so widely it looked scary.

"SING THE RAINBOW SONG AGAIN!" he yelled up at me. "SING IT FOR YOUR DADDY!"

And that's when everything broke.

All my words disappeared. I opened my mouth, but nothing came out. Not one word. Not one song. I just stood there in my pretty Dorothy dress with everyone in the whole town staring at me, and I couldn't remember anything.

The silence hurt my ears. The Scarecrow tried to help by saying something about Dorothy meeting a new friend, but I could tell he was scared too.

I could see Mommy in the audience. Her face looked pale, and she was pulling on Daddy's arm, trying to make him sit down. Leo was holding Rex super tight and looked like he might cry. Mrs. Henderson and some other grown-ups were rushing over.

And all the other parents, the normal ones whose daddies didn't get drunk and yell at plays, were staring at us. Some looked sorry for me. Some looked embarrassed, like they didn't want to watch but couldn't look away.

I knew what they were all thinking: Poor Olivia Parker. She's really good at singing, but look at her daddy. How awful.

I don't know how, but somehow I got through the rest of the play. The other kids had to whisper my lines to me when I forgot them. I moved around the stage like I was sleepwalking. When we finally got to the end and the curtain came down, people clapped, but it wasn't the same happy clapping from before. It was the kind of clapping grown-ups do when they feel sorry for you.

That made me feel worse than anything. I didn't want people to feel sorry for me. I wanted them to think I was amazing.

But now they just thought I was the girl with the drunk daddy who ruined the play.

Backstage was buzzing. Kids laughing, hugging, showing off costumes. Parents snapping pictures and gushing about how proud they were. But I sat in the corner still wearing my Dorothy dress, watching from the outside.

Leo found me there, Rex pressed tight against his chest. His eyes were wide.

"Livvy? Are you okay? You l-looked scared."

"I'm fine," I said, though my voice didn't sound like mine. Inside, something felt broken, like glass cracked down the middle.

"Daddy was really loud. Why was he so loud?"

"He was just... excited. Proud of me."

"But he made you f-forget your words."

That hit me harder than anything else. He was right. Daddy's pride, the loud, drunken kind, had ruined the one thing I'd wanted to get right more than anything in my life.

Parents began drifting over, their voices gentle and syrupy.

"You have such a beautiful voice, sweetheart.""Don't worry, you were wonderful.""Your father was just... very enthusiastic."

Each word cut. They were trying to be kind, but all I heard was pity. All I felt was the truth: everyone had seen. Everyone knew. And now they would always remember me as the girl whose drunk father ruined the play.

From across the room, I spotted Mommy near the back exit. She wasn't smiling politely or apologizing for Daddy like she usually did. She had him cornered against the wall, her back straight, her voice sharp enough that fragments carried over the noise.

"Bob, look at me. Look at what you just did to your daughter."

Daddy swayed, his eyes trying to focus. He looked lost, too drunk to understand the weight of her words.

"I was just... proud of her. So proud..."

"You were drunk. At her play. In front of everyone."

Mrs. Henderson moved toward them as if she wanted to smooth things over, but Mommy lifted her hand without even looking away from Daddy.

"Please give me a moment with my husband."

It wasn't a question. Mrs. Henderson backed off.

"Bob," Mommy said again, her voice quiet but strong, stronger than I'd ever heard it. "You promised me. You promised you wouldn't drink tonight."

"I just had a couple. To calm my nerves—"

"You ruined Olivia's night. The night she worked for, the night that should have been hers. You made it about you. About your drinking."

For a second, I saw something flicker in Daddy's face. Something like shame.

"Linda, I didn't mean—"

"I don't care what you meant. I care what you did." She stepped closer, and people were staring now, but she didn't care. "And I care that this is the last time you will ever do this to one of our children."

"Don't be so dramatic—"

"I'm not being dramatic. I'm being clear. We're going home. You're going to sleep this off. And tomorrow we'll talk about what happens next."

Daddy opened his mouth, but Mommy was already walking away.

She came straight to me, kneeling down until her face was level with mine. Her hands were trembling, but her voice was soft.

"Olivia, you were magnificent. Every person in that audience saw it. They saw how talented you are."

"But Daddy ruined it," I whispered.

"Daddy made a mistake. A big one. But that doesn't change what you did. You were perfect for forty-five minutes. Nothing he did can take that away."

She stood and pulled me up too, smoothing my wrinkled dress.

"Mrs. Henderson," Mommy said, turning to my teacher, "thank you for giving Olivia this chance. She worked so hard for it."

"Of course," Mrs. Henderson said quickly. "She was wonderful. Truly."

"She was," Mommy replied firmly, like she was willing it into truth. "And that's the part she'll remember."

The ride home felt endless, even though it was only fifteen minutes. The car was silent except for Daddy's voice, heavy with slurred apologies, and the sound of Mommy's hands gripping the steering wheel so tightly her knuckles looked white.

"I'm sorry, princess," Daddy kept saying from the passenger seat. His words dragged, too emotional now, the way they always did when the beer ran out. "I was just so proud. You were so good up there. So beautiful. So talented. I wanted everyone to know you were mine."

I stared out the window, refusing to give him anything back.

"You don't know what it feels like," he went on. "To have a daughter like you. So special. Better than I ever deserved."

I pressed my forehead against the cool glass and watched the streetlights blur past.

"Olivia," he begged. "Please don't be mad at me. Please. I love you so much. You're the best thing I ever did with my life."

The words hurt more than if he'd yelled. Because I knew he meant them. I knew he loved me. And I also knew he'd humiliated me in front of the entire town. Both things were true at once, and that was the part I couldn't bear.

When we got home, I didn't answer him. I went straight to my room and closed the door.

I sat on my bed still wearing the Dorothy dress. The curls Mommy had worked so carefully were lopsided now. The makeup was smudged around my eyes from holding back tears. In the mirror across the room, Dorothy still stared back at me. Dorothy with her gingham dress and red glitter shoes. Dorothy who could click her heels and go home.

Her home was safe. My home wasn't.

I pulled the scissors out of the top drawer of my dresser, the ones Mommy kept there for school projects. I spread the blue skirt across my lap and whispered, "There's no place like home."

But that wasn't true. Not for me. That was Dorothy's line. Dorothy had Auntie Em. Dorothy had love without shame. I had a drunk father in the next room.

The first snip through the fabric was when the sobs finally came. Loud, ugly sobs that shook my whole chest. I cut the sleeves off, crying harder with every slice. For the minutes, I had been perfect. For the empty seat that broke my heart. For the way the whole room had seen me fall apart.

"I hate you," I whispered into the fabric. "I hate you."

Blue gingham scraps fell like confetti onto the carpet. I kept cutting. The skirt. The bodice. The sash. Every piece that had made me feel special.

The ribbons went next. I yanked them from my hair and sliced them to pieces. I dug the sparkles off the ruby slippers with my fingernails until they were just plain shoes again.

By the time I was done, the floor was covered with Dorothy's remains. Bits of blue, red, and silver glitter scattered everywhere like broken glass. I sat in the middle of it in my slip, shaking, my face streaked with makeup and tears.

I whispered it then, the words that burned into me and never left: "There's no place like home. And I hate my home."

Fresh tears came. Because Dorothy had a home worth going back to, and I didn't. My home was a place where people who loved you could still hurt you. Where love and shame lived in the same body.

I cried until my throat was raw, until my chest ached. I cried because I thought being perfect would save me, and it hadn't.

A knock on my door made me freeze. Mommy's voice came through softly. "Olivia? Honey, are you okay?"

Panic shot through me. I couldn't let her see me sitting in a pile of shredded fabric and sequins. I scrambled, wiping my wet face with my hands, pushing the scraps into the trash can.

"I'm fine, Mommy."

"Are you sure? Olivia?"

I looked around at the wreckage, at my red eyes in the mirror, and felt something hard settle in my chest. A wall.

"I'm fine, Mommy."

"Can I come in?"

I had maybe half a minute. I shoved more fabric deep into the trash can, rubbed at my face until the makeup smeared into pale streaks. I yanked on my pajamas, pulled my hair loose, and looked one last time in the mirror. My eyes were swollen, my cheeks blotchy. But maybe she'd think I was just tired.

"I'm changing," I called. "I'll be out in a minute."

Her footsteps paused, then moved away.

I stood there in my pajamas, the trash can stuffed full of blue and red, my body still trembling. The room looked normal again. I didn't. But at least I could hide the difference.

I practiced in the mirror until my face looked right. Not broken. Not like I'd just spent an hour ripping Dorothy into scraps on my bedroom floor. Just calm. Maybe a little sad, like someone who'd had a long night, but steady enough that nobody would ask too many questions.

When I thought I had it down, I opened my door.

Mommy was at the kitchen table with a mug of tea, waiting. The steam curled up into her tired face, and the second she looked at me, I knew she could see the crying I'd tried to wash away.

"How are you feeling, sweetheart?"

"Fine," I said, keeping my voice smooth. Not too cheerful, not too broken.

"You were so good today," she said softly. "Even with... even with everything that happened, you were brilliant up there."

"Thank you." I sat across from her, folded my hands on the table the way I'd seen adults do when they wanted to look composed.

"Daddy feels terrible about what happened," she went on. "He didn't mean to—"

"I know," I said quickly. The words slid out easier than I thought they would. "It's okay, Mommy. These things happen."

She searched my face like she was trying to measure how deep the damage went, waiting for the meltdown she probably expected: the tears, the anger, the explosion of feelings any normal ten-year-old would have after being humiliated in front of the whole town.

But she wouldn't find that. I'd already buried it. All the tears, all the rage, all the shame. I'd stuffed it down in the trash can upstairs with the shreds of Dorothy's dress.

The next morning, Mrs. Morales found me at my locker before first period. She didn't say anything at first, just stood there with that patient look she always had, the one that signaled she could wait all day if necessary.

"I heard what happened at the play," she said finally. "From Mrs. Henderson. She wanted me to check on you."

"I'm fine," I said automatically, shoving books into my locker.

"Olivia." Her voice was soft but firm. "You don't always have to be fine."

My throat tightened. For a moment, I wanted to tell her everything. About the dress. About the shame. About how I'd smiled through the whole thing even though I wanted to disappear.

But I couldn't. So I just said, "It's over now. The play's done."

She nodded slowly. "My classroom is always open. Lunch, after school, whenever. You know that, right?"

"I know."

"Good." She touched my shoulder briefly. "Because you're allowed to feel things, Olivia. Even the hard things."

Then she walked away, leaving me standing there with tears I refused to let fall.

At school, when kids asked about Daddy shouting from the back row, I smiled and told them he'd just been excited to see me perform.

When Leo asked what happened to my costume, I shrugged and told him I didn't need it anymore.

And when Daddy brought flowers, his eyes wet with promises he'd never keep, I hugged him and said it was okay.

But late at night, when the house was finally quiet and I was the only one still awake, I pulled Grandpa's compass from my nightstand. I held it in my palm and watched the little needle quiver and settle, always finding north. Steady.

I wasn't Dorothy. I wasn't going to sing my way into some magical place over the rainbow where everything was better.

But I still had direction. I still had something that told me which way was up.

And someday, when I was old enough and strong enough to leave, I would follow that compass until I found a home where love didn't mean humiliation. A place where love kept you safe.

Chapter Five

The Birthday Party

S*PRING 2004*

"Livvy, look! We got invited!"

Leo burst through the front door, waving a piece of blue construction paper like it was a winning lottery ticket. His face was lit up in a way I hadn't seen in months. Not since before Daddy's last bender. Not since before Mommy started working double shifts.

I took the paper from his hands. It was covered in stickers: dinosaurs, race cars, and stars. The kind that came in those big sheets from the dollar store.

Jack Miller's Birthday Party!Saturday, April 20th, 2:00 PMFun Zone Arcade & PizzaPlease RSVP to Mrs. Miller

"It's at Fun Zone!" Leo bounced on his toes, his stutter completely gone in his excitement. "They have the racing games, the basketball hoops, and the ball pit and—"

"Leo, slow down." But I was smiling too. Fun Zone was the place every kid in Millfield dreamed about. The place where birthday parties happened if your parents had money. Giant arcade games that ate quarters. A jungle gym three stories tall. Pizza that actually tasted good, not like the cardboard kind from the school cafeteria.

We'd walked past it a hundred times, pressing our faces against the windows to watch other kids play. But we'd never been inside.

"Can we go?" Leo's eyes were huge and hopeful. "Please?"

I looked at the invitation again. Saturday was five days away. Mommy would be working. Daddy probably wouldn't even remember we existed. And we definitely didn't have money for a present.

But Leo was looking at me like I had the power to give him the moon.

"Yeah," I said. "We'll figure it out."

That night at dinner, I showed Mommy the invitation. She was eating standing up at the kitchen counter, too tired to even sit down after her shift.

"That's wonderful, baby." Her smile was thin, stretched too tight. "I'm so glad Jack invited you."

"Can we go?" Leo asked. "Please, Mommy?"

She looked at the date. Her face did that thing where she was calculating money in her head. I could see her adding up the bills, subtracting her paycheck, trying to find room for a birthday present we couldn't afford.

"I have to work Saturday," she said finally. "But maybe Daddy can take you."

Leo's face fell. We both knew what that meant: Daddy showing up drunk or not showing up at all. The party turning into another humiliation.

"What if someone else takes us?" I said quickly. "Maybe Jack's mom?"

Mommy looked relieved, like I'd solved a problem she didn't want to face. "You could call and ask."

I did. Mrs. Miller answered on the second ring, her voice bright and cheerful in a way that made our house feel even more gray and small.

"Oh, of course we can pick you up! We're happy to give you a ride."

"Thank you," I said, trying to sound like the kids who got rides to birthday parties all the time.

After I hung up, Leo grabbed my hands and spun me around the kitchen. For one perfect moment, we were just kids who'd been invited to a party. Not Bob Parker's children. Not the poor family everyone pitied. Just kids.

"What do we get for Jack?" Leo asked on Wednesday night. We were sitting on his bed, Rex the dinosaur between us like he was part of the planning committee.

"I don't know. What do you get someone who already has everything?"

Because that was the thing about Jack Miller. His dad worked at some office in Cleveland. His mom didn't work at all; she just volunteered at school and drove an SUV that looked brand new. Their house had a two-car garage, a basketball hoop in the driveway, and curtains that matched.

"We could make him something," Leo said.

"Make what?"

"I don't know. Something cool." He picked up Rex and made him dance. "Remember when we made Rex? Out of that old blanket and the buttons?"

I remembered. Mommy had helped us back when she still had energy for things like that. We'd cut, sewn, and stuffed him until he looked exactly right. Leo had named him Rex and slept with him every single night since.

"We could make Jack a dinosaur too," I said slowly. "But bigger. Like a toy he can actually play with."

Leo's whole face lit up. "With wheels! So it can roll!"

"Yeah. We could paint it and everything."

"It'll be the best present," Leo said, already bouncing with excitement. "Better than anything from a store. Because we made it."

I wanted to believe him. I wanted to believe that something homemade could compete with video games and expensive toys. But I also remembered standing in Kroger, watching Mr. Peterson look at me like I was trash.

Still, we had no money and five days. Making something was our only choice.

"Okay," I said. "Let's do it."

We spent every afternoon that week in the backyard behind our house. There were piles of scrap wood there, left over from when the landlord tried to fix the fence two years ago and gave up.

"This piece," I said, holding up a chunk that was sort of dinosaur-shaped if you squinted. "We can sand it down."

Leo found an old piece of sandpaper in Daddy's toolbox. We took turns rubbing the wood until our arms ached and the edges were smooth. We used bottle caps for wheels, the metal kind from beer bottles. I tried not to think about where they came from.

For paint, we had leftovers—green from when Daddy tried to paint the bedroom and quit halfway through, red from an old craft project, and black from something Mommy used years ago. We mixed the green and black to make a darker dinosaur green. Leo painted carefully, his tongue sticking out in concentration.

"The spikes need to be pointy," he said, adding little triangles down the back.

I glued the bottle caps to the bottom with Elmer's glue, the only kind we had. It took forever to dry, so we had to wait overnight between each step. But slowly, over five days, the dinosaur took shape.

By Friday night, it was done.

It was about as long as a football, painted dark green with red spikes and black eyes. The bottle cap wheels spun when you pushed it. The tail was a little crooked, the glue showed in spots, and the paint wasn't perfectly even.

But we'd made it. Together. With our own hands.

"It's perfect," Leo whispered, rolling it across his bedroom floor.

"Jack's gonna love it," I said.

I needed to believe that. I needed to believe that something made with love and effort could matter as much as something bought with money.

Leo fell asleep that night with his hand on the dinosaur, as if he were protecting it. Or maybe saying goodbye.

Saturday was sunny and warm, the kind of spring day that felt like the world was trying to be kind.

We didn't have wrapping paper, so we used the comics section from the Sunday newspaper. I folded it carefully, taped the edges, and tried to make it look intentional rather than desperate. Leo drew a birthday cake on the outside with crayons.

Mrs. Miller's SUV pulled up at 1:45, shiny and clean, taking up half the driveway. She was blonde and smiling, wearing jeans that probably cost more than Mommy's entire paycheck.

"Hop in!" she called through the window.

The SUV smelled like a new car and vanilla air freshener. The seats were leather. There were cupholders everywhere, a DVD player in the back, and everything was so clean I was afraid to touch anything.

Jack was in the backseat, playing a Game Boy. He looked up when we climbed in.

"Hey, Leo!"

"Hey!" Leo grinned, clutching our newspaper-wrapped present.

We drove through neighborhoods I'd only seen from the bus. Houses with two stories, attached garages, and lawns that were actually green. No broken-down cars on driveways. No peeling paint. No bars on the windows.

This was where Jack lived. This was normal for him.

Fun Zone was massive, with flashing lights and sounds and colors everywhere. As soon as we walked in, the smell hit me—pizza and popcorn and that specific arcade scent of carpet, quarters, and kid sweat.

"Whoa," Leo breathed.

Kids were everywhere, running, laughing, and playing. The arcade games beeped and chirped. Somewhere, someone won a jackpot, and tickets came streaming out like a paper waterfall.

"Everyone gets twenty dollars in tokens," Mrs. Miller said, handing us each a plastic cup filled with gold coins. "And pizza will be ready at three!"

Twenty dollars. In tokens. Just for games.

Leo looked at me like I'd just handed him a treasure chest.

"Go play," I said.

And he ran.

For two hours, we forgot we were poor.

We raced cars that actually moved on the screen. We shot basketballs that made satisfying swish sounds. We climbed through the jungle gym three stories up and slid down slides that went so fast my stomach dropped. We ate pizza that was hot, cheesy, and had pepperoni that actually tasted like meat.

Leo's face was red from running, his hair sticking up in all directions. He was laughing so hard at something Jack said that he couldn't catch his breath.

This was what being a kid was supposed to feel like.

Not worrying about money or Daddy's drinking or whether we'd have food for dinner. Just playing. Just being happy.

I wanted to freeze this moment forever.

"Time for presents!" Mrs. Miller announced.

Everyone crowded around a table covered in wrapped boxes. They were stacked high, decorated with bows, ribbons, and professional wrapping. Glossy paper in bright colors. Big boxes, small boxes, everything perfect.

Our newspaper-wrapped dinosaur looked so small in my hands.

"You wanna give it to him?" I asked Leo.

He nodded, suddenly shy.

We walked up together. Leo held out our present, his face a mix of hope and nervousness.

"Happy birthday, Jack."

"Thanks!" Jack took it, shaking it a little. "What is it?"

"Open it and see," I said.

He tore off the newspaper. The dinosaur sat in his hands, dark green and proud despite its crooked tail and visible glue.

"Whoa, a dinosaur! That's so cool!" Jack's voice was loud and genuine. He turned it over, spinning the bottle cap wheels. "Did you make this?"

"Yeah," Leo said, his stutter returning a little. "Me and Livvy. It t-took all week."

"That's awesome. Thanks, guys!"

Jack set it on the table and grabbed the next present—a big box wrapped in shiny blue paper. From his grandparents, probably. He tore into it, revealing a robot that looked like it cost more than our monthly rent.

Other kids pressed in, looking at the presents. The dinosaur sat there, off to the side, next to piles of video games, action figures, and expensive things in expensive boxes.

It looked so small. So homemade. So obviously out of place.

"Hey, check out the robot!" one kid shouted.

"Let me see the Game Boy games!"

"This remote control car is sick!"

Nobody mentioned the dinosaur.

Leo tugged at my sleeve. "Can we go play more games?"

"Yeah," I said. "Let's go."

An hour later, I went looking for the bathroom and passed the main table. The presents were spread out, toys everywhere. Jack was playing with the robot, making it walk and talk.

The dinosaur sat in the corner of the table.

And it was broken.

The tail had snapped off. One of the bottle cap wheels had come loose and rolled away. The glue hadn't held. The wood had been too soft.

I stood there staring at it, my chest tight.

Jack hadn't broken it on purpose. He'd probably tried to play with it, and it just... fell apart. Because we'd made it with scrap wood and old glue and hope, and hope wasn't strong enough to hold things together.

I picked up the tail piece. The break was clean, jagged. Fixable, maybe, if we had better glue. If we had real materials. If we had money.

"Olivia?" Mrs. Miller appeared next to me, her voice soft. "Everything okay, sweetheart?"

"Yeah." I put the tail back down. "I was just looking."

She glanced at the broken dinosaur, and something flickered across her face. Pity, maybe. Or embarrassment.

"You kids made that, didn't you? That was so creative."

Creative. The word adults used when they meant "cute but not actually good."

"Jack loved it," she continued, even though Jack was across the room playing with his robot and hadn't touched the dinosaur since it broke. "It's the thought that counts."

The thought that counts.

I heard what she wasn't saying: Your present wasn't good enough, but at least you tried.

"Thanks for having us," I said, my voice coming out flat.

"Of course, honey. Anytime."

But we both knew there wouldn't be an anytime. Kids like us didn't get invited to places like this. This was a one-time thing. Charity.

I went back to the arcade, but the lights were too bright now, and the sounds were too loud. I found Leo at the basketball game, his face still happy and flushed.

"Did you see Jack open all the presents?" he asked. "That robot was so cool!"

"Yeah," I said. "Really cool."

"Do you think he liked our dinosaur?"

I looked at my little brother, still believing that love and effort could be enough. Still thinking that making something with your own hands meant it mattered.

"He loved it," I lied.

Mrs. Miller drove us home as the sun was setting. Leo fell asleep in the backseat, his head against the window, exhausted and happy.

"Thank you for coming," Mrs. Miller said as we pulled into our driveway. She looked at our house—the peeling paint, the sagging porch, the yard with more dirt than grass. "Jack had a wonderful time."

"Thanks for inviting us," I replied.

I helped Leo out of the car. He was so tired I had to half-carry him up the porch steps.

Mommy wasn't home yet. Daddy was passed out in his chair, an empty bottle on the floor beside him. The house was dark and small and smelled of stale beer.

Four hours ago, we'd been in a world of arcade lights and pizza and presents that came in perfect boxes. Now we were home.

I got Leo into his pajamas and tucked him into bed. He was already half-asleep, smiling at some dream.

"That was the best day," he mumbled. "We should go there every week."

"Yeah," I whispered. "Every week."

But I knew we wouldn't. Couldn't. Kids like us got one day in that world, and then we went back to ours.

I thought about Jack's house with the two-car garage and the matching curtains. I thought about the robot that cost more than our monthly rent. I thought about our dinosaur, broken in the corner, made with love but not with money.

Love, effort, and hope weren't enough.

The only thing that mattered was money. Power. The kind of success that meant you never had to make presents out of scrap wood and beer bottle caps. The kind that meant your kids never felt small.

That night, after Mommy came home and checked on us before going to bed exhausted, I turned on my desk lamp and opened my math textbook.

I had a test on Monday. I'd been planning to study Sunday night, maybe get a B+ like usual.

But B+ wasn't good enough anymore. B+ was scrap wood and broken dinosaurs and pity from women in clean SUVs.

I needed perfect grades. Perfect test scores. Perfect everything.

Because perfect was the only way out.

I studied until 2 AM. Then 3 AM. My eyes burned and my head ached, but I kept going. Every equation I solved was a step away from that broken dinosaur. Every problem I mastered was a promise: Leo would never feel small again. Never watch something he made with love fall apart in someone else's hands.

Through the wall, I could hear Leo's soft breathing. Safe in sleep. Still believing the world was fair.

I'd protect that belief as long as I could. But I'd also build us an escape route.

The compass needle pointed north, steady and sure.

And I'd follow it, no matter what it cost.

After the birthday party, something changed in me.

School became my mission. Every assignment had to be flawless. Every test perfect. Every project polished until it shone. I threw myself into studying as if I were training for something vital. Like my life depended on it.

Because it did.

I immersed myself in it like I was training for the Olympics. Each assignment had to be flawless. Every test perfect. Every project polished until it shone. My bedroom became a command center: color-coded folders, schedules taped to the wall, every hour accounted for between school and bedtime. I checked out extra books from the library, rewrote essays until they were masterpieces, and completed assignments nobody even asked for.

One night, Mommy found me at the kitchen table, papers spread everywhere like battle plans. "Olivia, you don't have to work this hard," she said gently.

"I want to," I answered, and it was true. But it was more than wanting. I needed it. Being perfect wasn't just about school anymore. It was about survival.

By November, I was staying up past midnight almost every night, hunched over my desk while the house below me rattled with the sounds of my parents. Some nights it was loud, yelling, doors slamming, Daddy's heavy footsteps pacing from room to room.

Other nights it was quiet but worse, their low voices leaking up through the vents, full of worry and apology that felt heavier than fighting.

I couldn't let any of it in. Perfect grades required perfect focus. Perfect focus meant pretending nothing else existed but the books in front of me.

So, I built a system. When the noise downstairs became too sharp, I put on headphones and played classical music from an old CD I'd found at the library. The kind that made me feel serious, like a college kid. When I was so tired my eyelids wanted to shut, I splashed cold water on my face or did jumping jacks in the corner until my heart sped up again.

And when my chest started tightening with worry about my family, I whispered to myself that good grades were how I kept us safe. That if I stayed perfect, maybe Daddy would drink less. Maybe Mommy would smile more.

That night, I curled up in bed with my history book still open beside me. The pages smelled like paper and ink, the words blurring together as my eyes grew heavy.

Through my bedroom door came the sounds that told me it was safe to rest: Mommy humming softly while folding laundry, Leo in the living room sounding out spelling words one by one in his careful little voice, and Daddy in his chair with the television low, no bottles in sight.

For once, the house felt calm. Normal. Like a family should feel. And all because of one perfect algebra worksheet. Nobody would ever know I'd rewritten it in the basement, shivering on the concrete floor at midnight while my pencil scratched across the page.

It didn't matter. I told myself it was worth it. Every late night, every skipped meal, every time I forced my eyes to stay open when they wanted to close. If it kept the peace, if it made everything steady, then it was worth the effort.

I drifted to sleep, whispering to myself, "This is worth it. Whatever it takes."

But even in my dreams, I wasn't resting. I was writing, erasing, and double-checking my answers. I was still working to get everything just right.

Chapter Six

Thirty-Seven Days of Hope

Winter 2005–Spring 2006

It happened on a Thursday. Leo and I were at school, Mommy was working a double at the diner, and Daddy was home alone. That night, when she opened the jewelry box, her scream split the house.

"My ring! Where's my grandmother's ring?"

It wasn't just any ring. Her wedding ring had been handed down from her grandmother. Three generations of women had worn it. It was the only real treasure in our family, proof that love could survive hard times. Proof that people stayed together.

Gone.

"What ring?" Daddy slurred from the couch, beer in hand, eyes glassy.

"My wedding ring! The one I've worn every single day for sixteen years! Where is it?"

"I don't know what you're talking about."

But Leo and I knew. We looked at each other; no words were needed. Daddy had pawned it. Traded family history for a few bills in his pocket. Whiskey money.

"You sold it," Mommy whispered, her voice shaking like it couldn't hold the weight of the truth. "You stole my grandmother's ring and sold it for alcohol."

"Linda, I would never... you're being crazy."

"Then where is it, Bob? Where is the ring that was here yesterday?"

Daddy stared at her, confused, drunk, maybe too far gone to even remember what he'd done. And somehow that was worse. He'd stolen from us and didn't even have the memory of it.

The fight that followed wasn't loud with violence. It was worse. Mommy's voice cracked like glass as she repeated the same sentence over and over.

"You stole my grandmother's ring to buy drinks!"

Daddy just kept saying he didn't remember.

Leo and I hid in our room with pillows pressed over our ears. But I could still hear Mommy crying. Deep, wrenching sobs that sounded like something permanent breaking inside her chest. I knew then she had finally realized the man she married didn't exist anymore. He'd been replaced by someone who would sell her ring to keep drinking.

"Is Mommy gonna be okay?" Leo whispered from his bed, Rex squished in his arms.

"I don't know," I told him, my voice shaking. "I don't think any of us are gonna be okay."

That's when Mommy called Uncle Mike.

Uncle Mike was Daddy's older brother, an electrician with a steady job, a nice house in the suburbs, a wife and kids who looked like they belonged in magazines. He'd bailed us out before, bought Christmas presents when Daddy couldn't, and fixed our car when it died. He was the one tether to normal family life we had left.

The next morning, Uncle Mike showed up at our kitchen table with his phone in his hand. His jaw was tight, and his voice was deadly quiet.

"I stopped by the pawn shop on the way here," he said, holding out his phone. "That's Linda's ring in their display case, isn't it? Three little diamonds, passed down from her grandmother?"

Daddy squinted at the screen, his face cycling through confusion, then recognition, then shame, then back to blankness. "I... I don't remember..."

"You don't remember stealing your wife's wedding ring?" Uncle Mike's voice was low, controlled, scarier than yelling.

"I wouldn't do that. I'd never do that to Linda."

"But you did. And if you don't remember, it means you were blackout drunk when you traded your family's history for a few days of booze."

The silence was thick. I could hear the kitchen clock ticking. I could hear Leo's quick breaths as he held Rex tighter. Mommy stood at the counter, her hands clenched around nothing, holding herself together with sheer force.

"This is rock bottom, Bob," Uncle Mike said finally. "You've stolen from your wife, lied to your children, and lost your job because you can't stop drinking on company time. You've got a choice to make."

Daddy blinked, confused. "What choice?"

"Treatment or losing everything. And I mean everything. Linda already told me she will leave you. Your kids won't trust you. And the rest of us? We'll give up on you completely."

Daddy looked around the table then, at Mommy's bare finger, at Leo's scared eyes, at me, sitting there with my jaw tight, twelve years old and already old enough to know I'd never, ever be like him.

"If I go to treatment... if I get sober... you think Linda will take me back?" His voice was small, almost childlike.

Uncle Mike didn't blink. "It's your only chance and your last chance."

For the first time in months, something real flickered across Daddy's face. Not sobriety; he was still drunk from last night. But recognition. A flash of clarity, like he could see for one second the man he'd become.

"Okay," he whispered. "Okay. I'll go."

That night, I listened to Daddy packing a bag. Promises floated down the hallway about getting sober, about earning back our trust, about being the father we deserved.

Through the thin walls, I could hear him stumbling around, drawers slamming open and shut, his voice mumbling half-sentences. Every few minutes, it would go quiet, and I'd freeze, waiting to see if he'd passed out again or just lost track of what he was doing.

"Where's my... where did I put..." His voice dragged, then rose again. "Linda, have you seen my blue shirt?"

Mommy didn't answer. She was in the kitchen, phone pressed to her ear, talking about treatment centers and insurance and things that sounded heavy and complicated. The kinds of things kids weren't supposed to know about, but I couldn't stop listening through the hum of her voice.

Daddy's really going this time, I told myself. He has to. Uncle Mike said, "rock bottom." Mommy's ring was gone. There was nothing left to lose.

But then other memories pushed in. The plate shattering against the wall. The school play, his voice booming drunk from the back of the auditorium. Each time he had promised. Each time I had believed. And each time, it had all fallen apart again.

I tried to imagine it. Daddy's home from treatment, really sober this time. Pancakes on Saturday mornings again. Him helping Leo throw a baseball in the yard. Maybe even Christmas with lights and presents instead of pawn shops and yelling.

Please let this time be different, I whispered into the dark.

Outside, a car rolled by with music blasting, the bass thumping through the street. Normal teenager noise, not like the chaos that lived in our house. I listened until it faded.

The next morning, I woke to voices in the kitchen. Low and careful, like people trying not to wake anyone up.

I crept to the doorway and saw Daddy sitting at the table with the phone pressed to his ear. His hands were shaking. A cup of coffee sat untouched in front of him, steam rising into nothing.

"I don't know if I can do this, Richard," he said, his voice cracking.

A pause. Then: "Yeah, I know. You told me it would come to this."

Another long silence. I could hear a man's voice on the other end, steady and calm, though I couldn't make out the words.

"Twelve years?" Daddy said, his eyes wet. "You've really been sober twelve years?"

More talking from the other end. Daddy nodded like the person could see him.

"Linda wants me to go to Serenity Hills. She says she'll file for divorce if I don't." His voice dropped to almost nothing. "I pawned her grandmother's ring, Richard. I don't even remember doing it."

The voice on the phone grew louder and more insistent. I heard it rise and fall, patient yet firm.

"I'm scared," Daddy whispered. "What if I can't do it? What if thirty days isn't enough?"

Whatever Richard said next made Daddy's whole body sag with relief. His shoulders dropped. He wiped his eyes with the back of his hand.

"You'd really come to meetings with me when I get out?"

A pause.

"Every week?"

Another pause, longer this time.

"Okay," Daddy said finally. "Okay. I'll go. But you have to promise you'll be there when I come back. I can't do this without someone who understands."

The voice on the other end said something brief. Something that sounded like a promise.

"Thanks, Richard. I mean it. Thanks."

He hung up and sat there for a long time, staring at the phone as if it had just saved his life.

I backed away before he could see me, my heart pounding. I didn't know who Richard was, but his voice had done something I'd never seen anyone do before.

It made Daddy believe he could get better.

Serenity Hills took him in on a gray December morning. He looked smaller than I'd ever seen him, shoulders hunched like he was trying to fold into himself. Uncle Mike drove him there. Mommy couldn't go. She was working a double at the diner, and Leo and I walked into school pretending it was a normal day.

"How long will D-Daddy be gone?" Leo asked that night, his stutter sharper, as if fear made the words stick harder in his throat.

"As long as it takes," Mommy said. But her voice didn't match the words. I could tell she didn't believe it would work. Not really.

This time did feel different, though. Daddy had stolen Mommy's wedding ring. Uncle Mike had looked him dead in the eye and said, "rock bottom." This time, Leo seemed scared in a way I hadn't seen before, like he knew what would happen if treatment didn't stick.

The first week felt like someone had lifted a heavy blanket off our house. No stomping feet in the hallway and no bottles clinking into the trash.

Just silence and peace.

"I can breathe better," Leo told me one night at the kitchen table, pencil in his hand, spelling words neatly across his paper. "Like the air in our house isn't thick anymore."

He was right. Without Daddy's drinking, everything felt lighter. Mommy's face softened. Leo's stutter eased. I could fall asleep without lying awake listening for trouble in the living room.

But peace didn't pay for medicine.

One evening, Mommy shook Leo's inhaler and frowned. "It's low," she said quietly. "We need to refill it, but the co-pay's thirty-five dollars. I don't have it until Friday."

"How low?" I asked, my stomach knotting.

"Three, maybe four days left."

But Leo didn't know how to ration. He reached for his inhaler when his chest got tight, or when recess made his lungs work too hard, or when worry about Daddy's drinking made it feel like he couldn't get air. By Thursday morning, it barely rattled.

"Leo, you've gotta make it last," I told him.

"I'm trying," he wheezed, already pale. "But it's hard to breathe."

Friday came. No paycheck. The diner was behind. Saturday came. Leo took tiny puffs, stretching what wasn't there. Sunday morning, it was empty.

"We'll refill it first thing Monday," Mommy promised. But her eyes said something different.

That night, Leo woke me at two a.m. "Livvy," he whispered, his voice raw. "I can't breathe right."

The sound of his chest rattling in the dark made my blood run cold. Each breath was shallow, like he was pulling air through a straw.

"Where's your inhaler?" I asked, though I already knew.

"It's gone."

By morning, his lips were tinged blue. His whole body strained just to breathe.

"Mommy!" I shouted.

She was in the kitchen, her coat already on. One look at Leo and she grabbed her keys. "Emergency room. Now."

The twenty-minute drive to Cleveland Metro felt endless. I sat in the backseat holding Leo's hand while he gasped for air, my heart pounding like it might burst.

"It's okay, Leo," I kept whispering. "Almost there. You're gonna be okay."

But in his eyes, I saw the same question I was asking myself. What if this was the big one?

At the ER, nurses hooked him to a nebulizer. The hiss of medicine filled the room, and his chest rose and fell a little easier with each minute. Steroids followed, and finally, the gray left his face. Relief washed through me so fast my knees shook.

But then the doctor spoke. "He needs his prescription refilled immediately. We're also adding a daily controller medication to prevent attacks like this."

Mommy's voice was small. "How much?"

"About two hundred for the rescue inhaler. One fifty a month for the controller."

Two hundred dollars might as well have been two thousand. We didn't have twenty.

The pharmacy tech tried to be kind. "We can do a payment plan, but we need at least fifty percent down."

One hundred dollars. Still impossible.

I watched Mommy's face as she did the math out loud, trying to pull money from places that didn't exist. Leo sat in the plastic chair beside her, clutching Rex, breathing a little steadier but still fragile.

Finally, she whispered, "I'll have to make a call."

I knew before she said it who she meant. Uncle Mike. The one she hated leaning on, the one who had already bailed us out more times than I could count.

She stared at the phone like it was a loaded weapon. "I don't want to call him," she said, shame tightening her voice. "But Leo needs it."

"I'll call him," I said.

"Olivia, you shouldn't have to—"

"Mom, Leo can't breathe, and we don't have money. I'll call Uncle Mike."

My hands shook as I dialed, the plastic buttons slippery under my fingers. I prayed he would pick up, prayed he wouldn't be too angry with Daddy to help us, prayed he'd remember that Leo and I still deserved to be saved even if Daddy didn't.

"Uncle Mike? It's Olivia."

"Olivia? What's going on? You sound upset."

And then the dam broke. Everything I'd been carrying for weeks, months, maybe years spilled out of me in one desperate rush.

"Leo can't breathe, and we're at the hospital, and we don't have the two hundred dollars for the emergency room and the medication. We don't have it because Daddy's in treatment, and Mommy's paycheck is late, and we couldn't refill his prescription, and I don't know what to do."

The words tumbled between sobs, my twelve-year-old body shaking with the weight of being too responsible for too long.

"Slow down, sweetheart," Uncle Mike said gently. "Take a breath. Where are you?"

"Cleveland Metro. The emergency room."

"I'll be there in thirty minutes."

When he walked in, he carried two things: cash in his wallet and fury in his eyes. He paid for Leo's medications without blinking, but his gaze kept scanning, taking inventory of what our family had become: Mommy's face lined with exhaustion, Leo pale and clutching Rex, me hollow-eyed from lack of sleep.

"Bob's still at Serenity Hills?" he asked flatly.

"Yes," Mommy said, her voice tight.

"And meanwhile his son nearly dies because Bob didn't save thirty-five dollars for an inhaler refill?"

"Mike, please—"

"No, Linda. This is exactly what I've been saying. Bob's drinking doesn't just wreck his own life. It creates chaos that keeps hurting everyone around him, even when he's supposedly getting better."

Later, in the car, his tone softened for Leo. "How long was your inhaler empty, buddy?"

"Since Sunday," Leo whispered.

"And how did that feel? Not being able to breathe right?"

"Scary. Really scary."

"I'll bet it was." Uncle Mike's eyes were damp, but his voice stayed steady. "Listen to me. That wasn't your fault. Not having your medicine? That's an adult problem, not a kid problem."

I could see, though, how worried he was about money. Without Daddy working, we were sinking fast. The treatment that was supposed to save our family was also draining our finances.

"This can't go on, Linda," he said on the drive back. "You're working yourself into the ground just to keep this family afloat while Bob's away. You can't carry it all."

"I don't have a choice."

"You do." His voice was quiet but firm. "You just don't want to acknowledge it yet."

I didn't understand then what he meant. But I would soon enough.

When Daddy finally came home after thirty-seven days, he looked like a different man. Lighter. Smaller. Sober in a way that made his eyes clearer than I'd ever seen. His hair was trimmed, his clothes fit better, and his voice had that careful, deliberate quality of someone learning how to live without numbing himself.

"I'm sorry," were his first words. No excuses. No deflection. Just a raw apology.

"I'm sorry for stealing your ring, Linda. I'm sorry that Leo ended up in the hospital while I was gone."

He meant it. At least in that moment.

He picked up a job at the gas station on Route 9. Not glamorous, but steady. The kind of place that would fire you the moment you smelled like alcohol. He went to AA meetings every morning before work and every evening after dinner. He brought home pamphlets and readings about recovery, leaving them in plain sight like he wanted us to know he wasn't hiding anymore.

And then there was Richard.

Richard Kowalski. The man whose voice I'd heard on the phone that morning before treatment, talking Daddy down from the edge. The one who'd promised to be there when Daddy came home.

He kept that promise.

Richard was Daddy's sponsor. A carpenter with twelve years sober, the kind of steady man Daddy might've been if alcohol hadn't hollowed him out. He drove a blue pickup that showed up in our driveway every Wednesday and Friday, just like he'd said he would. He never honked. He always walked to the door, shook Daddy's hand, and treated the whole thing like a ritual.

"How was your day?" I heard him ask once when I answered.

"Good," Daddy said, shoulders squared. "I worked my shift, came home to my family, didn't think about drinking once."

"That's it," Richard replied, clapping him on the back. "One good day at a time."

Sometimes he came inside, sitting at our table while Mommy asked about meetings or the job. He never made us feel like a case file. He just treated us like people, like we mattered.

For three weeks, Richard's visits were the steadiest part of our lives. Every Wednesday and Friday without fail.

"Richard says the first year is the hardest," Daddy told me one evening, his voice hopeful. "But if you make it through, you start to remember who you were before the drinking."

I looked at him, really looked at him. "Who were you before?"

"I was going to be a carpenter," Daddy said one night, his voice soft as if he were admitting a secret. "Before I met your mother, before the drinking got bad, I wanted to build houses. Richard says it's not too late to learn."

Those weeks with him sober felt like borrowed time, like someone had pressed pause on the chaos that had defined my childhood. Daddy went to work, came home steady, talked about building things instead of breaking them. And Richard, faithful, dependable Richard, showed up every Wednesday and Friday, proof that maybe recovery was possible.

Which is why what happened next crushed us.

The call came on a Monday in late January. Richard, the man who'd been sober for twelve years and had become a lifeline for Daddy, was found dead in his blue pickup truck outside Home Depot. Heroin overdose. A needle in his arm.

Daddy was devastated by the loss. "Twelve years," Daddy said when he got the news, his voice hollow. "Twelve years sober, and he dies like that."

"Bob, that doesn't mean—" Mommy tried, but he cut her off.

"What's the point, Linda? What's the point of trying so hard if even twelve years of sobriety doesn't save you?"

I saw it then. The look I dreaded most. That sad, hopeless vacancy that always came before he picked up a bottle.

"Richard dying doesn't mean sobriety doesn't work," Mommy pressed.

"Doesn't it?" he snapped. "If a man like Richard couldn't stay clean forever, what chance do I have?"

That night he paced until three in the morning, muttering about failure, about being too broken to fix. The next evening, he didn't come home from his AA meeting. The evening after that, still nothing.

By Thursday, Uncle Mike was calling every hour, and Mommy was back on the phone with bars and friends and anyone who might have seen him. "Nobody's seen him," she kept saying, her voice getting thinner each time. "It's like he disappeared."

We found him Friday evening in Mommy's bedroom, sprawled across her jewelry box. He was digging through the empty compartments, mumbling about her wedding ring.

"Where is it?" he slurred, hands shaking. "I need to find Linda's ring."

"Bob," Mommy said from the doorway, her voice already broken. "The ring is gone. You sold it two months ago."

"No, I didn't. I'd never..."

He looked up, his eyes lost and confused, and I understood something terrifying. He didn't remember. He wasn't lying to us to cover it up. He genuinely had no memory of pawning it.

"I need to find that ring," he insisted, going back to searching the empty box.

That was the moment I knew we'd lost him. Not to death yet, but to the disease that had hollowed him out from the inside.

Uncle Mike showed up an hour later, taking in the sight of Daddy passed out, clutching the empty jewelry box.

"He doesn't remember," he said quietly. "That's late-stage alcoholism. The brain just... stops recording. He could've done anything this past month and have no idea."

I looked at Daddy lying there, still searching in his sleep for something he'd already destroyed, and it hit me like a blow: we weren't dealing with bad choices anymore. We were dealing with a sickness stronger than his love for us.

That was the last straw.

"This is the last time," Uncle Mike said, his voice sharp with finality. "I won't enable him anymore. Linda, you need to protect yourself and the kids."

"Protect us from what?" Mommy whispered.

"From the end," he said. "Because people in Bob's condition don't usually make it. They drink until they die, or until their families walk away."

That night, Leo and I heard Mommy making hushed calls from the kitchen. Lawyers, custody, plans for a life on the other side of Daddy's disease.

"Are Daddy and Mommy getting divorced?" Leo asked me in the dark.

"I think so."

"Is it because of me? Because I cost too much money when I got sick?"

"No," I told him firmly. "It's because Daddy's too sick to choose us over drinking anymore."

"Will he be okay by himself?" he whispered.

I didn't know how to answer. The truth was that he probably wouldn't, but that was too heavy for a ten-year-old.

"I don't know," I said. "But I know we can't save him. And trying is making us all sick too."

Six months later, we were in a small apartment across town. We were asked to visit Daddy on weekends at our old house where he still lived. But in our new, quiet space, miracles happened. Leo's stutter eased. Mommy's smile returned. And for the first time in years, I remembered what it felt like to be a child instead of the family's crisis manager.

One evening, a few weeks after we'd settled in, I found Mommy standing at the kitchen sink, staring at her bare left hand.

"Uncle Mike called today," she said without looking up. "He went back to the pawn shop."

My chest tightened. "The ring?"

"Already sold. Some woman bought it three days after your father pawned it." She turned the faucet on, then off again, still staring at her empty finger. "Mike offered to buy me a new one. He said I deserved something to replace what Bob took."

"What did you say?"

She was quiet for a long moment. Then she held up her hand, fingers spread, the pale band of skin where the ring used to be already starting to fade.

"I told him no. That ring was supposed to mean forever. Three generations of women wore it, believing in promises that would last." She dropped her hand. "But forever ended the day Bob traded our family history for whiskey. And I don't need a replacement to remind me of that."

"So you're just not going to wear one?"

"Not right now." She finally looked at me, and her eyes were clear. Sad, but clear. "Maybe someday I'll want a ring that means something new. Something I chose for myself, not something handed down with expectations I couldn't meet. But right now, this empty space reminds me I'm free."

She went back to washing dishes, and I watched the light catch on her bare finger, thinking about how sometimes the absence of something can mean more than its presence ever did.

Chapter Seven

Rex and the Beer Bottles

F ALL 2007

The smell hit before we even crossed the threshold. Not just beer, though that was everywhere, but cigarette smoke layered thick over something rotting I couldn't quite identify. A smell that felt like a warning. It was our first court-ordered weekend visit since the custody papers were signed. Stepping into our old house felt less like going home and more like walking into a place where hope had already abandoned.

"It's... really different in here," Leo whispered.

Different didn't even begin to cover it. The living room that had once held family dinners and bedtime stories had transformed into something collapsing in on itself.

Daddy's recliner, the same chair where he'd once read *Green Eggs and Ham*, was now sunk deep with stains, scarred with cigarette burns. Empty bottles covered every surface, lined the baseboards like soldiers, sentinels of his addiction standing guard.

"Sorry about the mess, kids," Daddy said, shuffling in from the kitchen with a beer already in his hand, even though it wasn't yet ten in the morning. "Been meaning to clean, but work's been keeping me busy."

The lie slipped out of him so easily I almost wondered if he believed it. There was no work. There was only this house, decaying around him, while he drank.

"Where should we put our overnight bags?" I asked, though the question felt surreal. Like asking where to pitch a tent in a dump.

"Your old room's just like you left it," he said with pride, as if that was a comfort.

It wasn't.

The twin beds were there, sure, but the sheets hadn't been changed since we'd moved out. They were gray with grime, stiff with stains. The air was thick, sour with mildew.

"We can't sleep here," I whispered to Leo.

"Where else?"

"Maybe the couch."

But the couch was worse. Ash, beer stains, something dried that looked like vomit. In the end, we sat up in our room all night, fully clothed, trying to breathe through our mouths. Leo pressed close to me, Rex tucked beneath his arm like a shield.

"It's like camping," he said bravely. "Like roughing it in the woods."

"Yeah," I said, forcing a smile. "Camping."

But camping was supposed to be chosen. Camping wasn't watching your father rot in a place that smelled like despair.

The kitchen was worse.

Dishes stacked high in the sink, food cemented to them like plaster. The refrigerator was a biology experiment gone bad. Cartons of milk turned to sludge, and lunch meat curled green at the edges. Mouse droppings dusted the counters, and when I opened a cabinet, I caught the flick of a mouse tail.

"Hungry? I'll make you breakfast," Daddy said, rooting through the cabinets.

"We're not really hungry," I lied, my stomach twisting.

"Come on, princess. Let me fry you some eggs and pancakes. Like old times."

"The stove doesn't look safe. Maybe just cereal?"

He grinned like it was the best idea he'd heard in years. "Cereal it is!"

We ate it dry, avoiding eye contact, pretending this was normal.

The contrast between his world and Mommy's felt violent. At her apartment, life had rhythm: dinners at the table, clean sheets at night, air that smelled like vanilla candles instead of stale smoke. With Daddy, every weekend was survival. Breathing foul air, skirting broken furniture, pretending not to see what was killing him.

"How was your weekend?" Mommy asked every Sunday when Uncle Mike dropped us back.

"Fine," I said. Automatic.

"Fine," Leo echoed, though I saw the slump of his shoulders, the way two days of watching Daddy disintegrate aged him past twelve.

And Daddy's desperation kept seeping through.

"I miss you kids so much," he'd tell us, his voice heavy with self-pity. "This house is so empty without you. Sometimes I sit in your old room and cry."

"We miss you too, Daddy," Leo always answered quickly, because he still believed love could patch the holes alcohol had carved.

"Do you? Or are you happier with your mother? In that nice apartment? With no smell of beer? No embarrassing father?"

"We're not embarrassed by you," Leo insisted. Half true. Half a lie.

Then came the words that froze me:

"Sometimes I think about giving up. Sometimes I think you'd all be better off if I just... stopped trying."

Daddy started talking about giving up. Not just giving up drinking, but giving up living. The words came out late at night or in the middle of our visits, heavy and hopeless, and they scared Leo so much he would spend the whole weekend trying to hold Daddy together.

"Don't say that, Daddy. We need you. We love you. We want you to get better."

"But what's the point of getting better if my own family doesn't want to be around me?"

"We do want to be around you. That's why we're here."

"Only because a judge makes you come. If you had a choice, you'd never see me again."

The conversations never ended. They just circled the drain, with Leo trying to prove his love and Daddy twisting it into proof of how much he was suffering. I hated those talks. They felt like traps, like Daddy was using Leo's love as a bandage for wounds he kept reopening himself. But Leo was twelve, still too young to tell the difference between real sadness and the kind of sadness that was meant to make us feel guilty.

While Daddy was sinking deeper, Mommy was turning into someone new.

It started small. Like the first time she hung up on him when he called drunk at nine o'clock at night, demanding to talk to us even though we had school the next morning.

"Bob, you're intoxicated and it's past the kids' bedtime. Call back tomorrow when you're sober."

Click.

"That seemed mean," Leo whispered, eyes wide.

"It wasn't mean," Mommy said, calm and steady. "It was a boundary. Your father doesn't get to ruin our evening because he's lonely and drunk."

Her strength kept building from there.

One Saturday, Uncle Mike pulled into the driveway and found Daddy passed out on the porch at two in the afternoon. In the old days, Mommy would've made excuses, said Daddy was tired or stressed or not feeling well. That day she didn't flinch.

"He's drunk, Mike. That's where he is."

Uncle Mike frowned. "The kids don't have to see him like this."

"The court order says weekend visits," Mommy said. "If Bob chooses to be unconscious during his visitation time, that's his problem to solve."

Every time she said no, every time she refused to cover for him, something in her grew stronger. And for the first time, I began to see how much of our lives had been swallowed up by making excuses for him.

My answer to the split-custody chaos was simple: disappear into schoolwork.

Millfield High was a clean slate. None of the teachers knew my father's reputation. None of the students had seen him drunk in public. I could reinvent myself here as the smart, ambitious girl instead of the daughter of Bob Parker.

I signed up for every advanced class on the schedule: honors English, accelerated math, early chemistry, AP history. My transcript looked like it belonged to a kid aiming for college three years too early.

"Are you sure you can handle this much coursework?" Mrs. Franklin, my guidance counselor, asked during orientation.

"I thrive under pressure," I said. And in a way, it was true. Pressure was the only environment I'd ever lived in.

Homework became my hiding place. The kitchen table turned into a war room of textbooks and color-coded folders. I wrote essays late into the night, memorized French vocabulary while brushing my teeth, and worked through calculus problems until the numbers blurred. Schoolwork was clean and logical. Effort went in, results came out. No surprises.

Not like home. Not like loving someone who always picked alcohol first.

"You're always studying," Leo said one night, half admiring, half annoyed.

"I like studying."

"You like hiding."

He wasn't wrong. Homework was my Fort Rex now. A place to disappear when reality was too heavy to carry.

But while I was burying myself in books, Leo was drowning in guilt.

"It's my fault Mom and Dad got divorced," he whispered one night in our room.

"How could it be your fault?"

"Because my asthma medicine costs so much. If I wasn't sick, maybe they wouldn't have fought about money."

"Leo, no. Mom and Dad didn't get divorced because of you. They divorced because Daddy chose drinking over everything else."

"But what if I hadn't gotten sick that day? What if Uncle Mike hadn't had to pay for my medicine? Maybe Dad wouldn't have felt so guilty. Maybe he wouldn't have drunk so much—"

"Stop." I sat up and looked him straight in the eye. "Dad's drinking is not your fault. It started long before you ever had asthma. It would've happened no matter what."

"But maybe if I was less expensive—"

"Leo, Daddy didn't pawn Mom's wedding ring because of your medical bills. He pawned it because he needed money to drink. The hospital trip just made it obvious how far he was willing to go."

But I could see it in his face that he didn't believe me. At twelve years old, he carried the impossible idea that being cheaper, easier, and better might somehow save our family.

And I didn't know how to take that weight out of his hands.

By Christmas, money had run out so completely that I had to join the fight to keep us afloat.

Mommy was working herself ragged. Double shifts at the diner, feet swollen by the time she got home, hands raw from scrubbing counters. But tips and waitress wages weren't enough to cover rent, utilities, and food for three people. Daddy's child support was either missing entirely or funneled into court-ordered counseling sessions he only showed up for half the time.

"I can get a job," I told her one night. She was at the kitchen table with stacks of bills spread out in front of her like evidence in a trial we were already losing.

"Olivia, you're fourteen," she said, not looking up. "You should be focusing on school and being a kid."

"I can do both. Morrison's Grocery hires kids with working papers. Fifteen hours a week. Weekends."

"I don't want you working. That's my job, taking care of this family."

"You're already doing everything you can. And it's not enough. We need the money."

And just like that, I became the teenager bagging groceries while my classmates hung out at the mall or went to movies. Fifteen hours at minimum wage came out to about $120 every two weeks. I gave Mommy a hundred for bills and kept twenty for myself. More than I'd ever held in my own hands, earned without stealing or begging. It felt like independence, responsibility, and adulthood all wrapped into a thin pay envelope. It also felt like something no fourteen-year-old should have to understand.

Meanwhile, Daddy's emergencies became a constant rhythm in our lives.

Every few weeks, Uncle Mike would call with updates. Alcohol poisoning after a binge. Pneumonia from living in a house without heat. A concussion from falling down his steps drunk.

"Bob's back at Cleveland Metro," Uncle Mike would say, his voice flat with the exhaustion of someone who'd made this call too many times. "Dehydration and malnutrition this time. They're keeping him overnight."

The cycle was always the same: hospital stay, shaky apologies, dramatic promises to quit, a few days of shaky sobriety, then the slide back into drinking until the next crisis.

"I'm done this time," Daddy would tell us from his hospital bed, IV in his arm, face pale and hollow. "Really done. I thought about you kids while I was lying here. I can't put you through this anymore."

And for a few days, maybe a week, he'd sound almost believable. He'd shower, shave, maybe even try to clean the house. He'd call us with stories about how he was turning things around. But it never lasted. The promises got emptier each time, and the sober stretches shorter.

Hospital. Apology. Hope. Relapse. Repeat.

"I don't understand," Leo said after the fifth hospitalization that year. "He keeps saying he'll stop. But he always starts again."

"He can't stop," I said, the words sharp in my mouth. "Not won't. Can't. The disease is stronger than his love for us now."

"That's not true."

"It is. And the sooner you believe it, the less it'll hurt every time he breaks another promise."

"But what if this time is different?"

"He probably means it every time," I said. "But meaning it and doing it are two completely different things when you're this far into addiction."

By spring, my resentment had hardened into something cold and sharp. I was done with hospital vigils and fake promises. Done with weekend visits where Leo cried every Sunday night and I went home feeling like I'd aged another year. Done carrying the weight of Daddy's failures on my back.

"He's choosing this," I told Mommy after one weekend when we'd found him passed out in his own vomit.

"Olivia, it's not that simple. Addiction is a disease—"

"I know. But diseases have treatments. And he refuses every single one. He checks out of rehab early. Skips AA. Ignores doctors. He's sick, but he's also giving up. And I'm tired of pretending our visits help him when they just make it easier for him to keep living like this."

She looked at me for a long moment, her face lined and tired. Then she nodded. "You're right. And that's exactly why we had to leave."

The repetition finally broke in early June, and not in a way I ever expected.

Leo had been quiet all weekend, slipping out to the garage while Daddy drank himself through Friday and Saturday. I thought he was avoiding the house, the smells, the chaos. I didn't realize he was unraveling in his own way.

When Uncle Mike came Sunday to take us home, Leo was gone.

"Leo!" I called, panic rising as I searched the kitchen, the bathroom, our old hiding spots. Nothing.

"Maybe he's still in the garage," Daddy said, cigarette dangling, beer in hand.

But the garage was empty.

That's when I heard it. A low, steady snore coming from the living room.

Not Daddy's. He was right there, awake.

I walked back in and saw my twelve-year-old brother slumped in Daddy's recliner. Head tilted back, mouth open, face slack. A beer bottle lay on the floor beside him, still dripping foam. Another one, empty, sat on the side table.

For one sickening moment, I couldn't breathe.

The room tilted sideways. My vision narrowed to just Leo's face, that slack expression I'd seen a hundred times before but never on him. The smell of beer mixed with something sour hit me, and suddenly I was six years old again, standing in a doorway in duck pajamas, watching Daddy's body shake on cold bathroom linoleum.

The same position. The same smell. The same terrifying stillness between breaths.

My legs moved without permission. I stumbled forward, reaching for Leo's shoulder, but my hands wouldn't work properly. They shook so badly I couldn't grip him. I tried to shake him awake, but it felt like my body had forgotten how to function.

"Leo," I whispered, but the word came out strangled. "Leo, wake up."

Nothing. His chest rose and fell too slowly, the same shallow breathing I remembered from Easter Sunday 1999. My stomach twisted. Bile burned in my throat.

This is how I lose him.

The thought slammed into me with such force I had to grab the armrest to stay upright. Not someday. Not eventually. Right now. Right here in this chair that reeked of Jack

Daniel's and cigarettes. I was watching my little brother cross a line we could never come back from.

"Oh my God," Uncle Mike whispered, rushing past me. "Leo. Leo, wake up."

He shook Leo's shoulder. Leo's head lolled to the side, but his eyes didn't open.

"What's wrong?" Daddy asked, coming up behind us with a beer still in his hand, his face confused. "Why is everyone looking at Leo like that?"

"Bob, your son is passed out drunk," Uncle Mike said, his voice tight.

Daddy blinked, like the words didn't compute. "What? No, no, he's just sleeping. Kids that age sleep deep."

"He reeks of beer. And there are two empty bottles next to him."

Uncle Mike kept shaking Leo's shoulder, harder now. "Leo. Leo, buddy, wake up."

Leo's eyelids fluttered. He made a small sound, somewhere between a groan and a whimper.

"Come on, Leo. Open your eyes."

Finally, Leo's eyes cracked open. Unfocused. Glassy. He looked around like he didn't know where he was.

Then, his face went green.

"He's gonna be sick," I said.

Uncle Mike grabbed him under the arms and half-carried, half-dragged him to the bathroom. The sounds that followed made my stomach turn. Leo retching, crying, the whole time Uncle Mike murmuring, "It's okay, get it out, that's it."

I stood in the hallway, frozen. Behind me, Daddy was saying something about how it was just a couple of beers, no big deal; kids needed to learn their limits somehow.

"He's twelve years old, Bob!" Uncle Mike shouted from the bathroom. "Twelve! And he's so drunk he couldn't wake up!"

"He only had one beer," Daddy said, defensive now. "Maybe two. That's nothing for a kid his size."

"For a kid his size, that's enough to make him sick as a dog and pass out. That's not nothing!"

When Leo finally stopped throwing up, Uncle Mike brought him out. His face was chalk-white, his legs shaky. He couldn't stand without leaning on Uncle Mike.

"We're taking him to the ER," Uncle Mike said.

"He doesn't need the ER," Daddy muttered. "He just needs water and sleep."

"Bob," Uncle Mike's voice went deadly quiet. "Your twelve-year-old son just drank himself unconscious. We're taking him to the hospital."

In the car, Leo came around a little more. Still groggy, still green, but awake enough to cry.

"I'm sorry," he whispered, his voice so small it barely filled the car. "I'm so sorry."

"What were you thinking?" I asked, sharper than I meant to. My fear had curdled into anger. "Why would you drink Daddy's beer?"

He looked down at his hands. "I wanted to understand. I wanted to know why Daddy chooses it over us. I thought if I tried it, maybe I'd figure out how to make him stop."

Twelve years old. Twelve, and already believing he had to solve the unsolvable. Already searching for answers in the same poison that had destroyed our father.

"It doesn't work that way," I said, my throat tight. "Drinking doesn't help you understand him. It doesn't fix anything."

"But what if I'm different? What if I can handle it better than he does?"

The question sliced through me because I'd wondered the same thing. Whether it was weakness or genetics, whether someone like me, smart enough, strong enough, could drink without falling the way he had.

"Leo," I said finally, "addiction doesn't care if you're weak or strong. It's not about willpower. It's about your brain, about things you can't control just by trying harder. You can't gamble with this."

He didn't answer. He just cried.

At the ER, they took Leo back right away. The nurse asked questions about how much he'd had, how long he'd been unconscious, and whether this had happened before. Uncle Mike answered while I sat with Leo, holding his hand.

The doctor came in after they'd given Leo fluids and something for the nausea. She was young, maybe thirty, with tired eyes that said she'd seen this before.

"He's going to be okay," she said. "He's dehydrated, and his blood alcohol is elevated, but not dangerously so. We'll keep him a few hours for observation to make sure he can keep fluids down."

"So he's not... it's not serious?" I asked.

"It's serious," she said firmly. "Just not immediately life-threatening. But I need you to understand something." She looked at Leo, then at Uncle Mike and me. "Any amount of alcohol is dangerous for a child. His body isn't equipped to process it the way an adult's is. What would make a grown man tipsy can make a child his age blackout drunk. He's lucky he didn't choke on his own vomit."

Leo's face crumpled.

"More than that," the doctor continued, "children who start drinking this young are far more likely to develop dependency later, especially if there's family history." She paused. "Is there family history?"

"Yes," Uncle Mike said quietly. "His father is an alcoholic."

The doctor nodded like she'd expected as much. "Then Leo's risk isn't just elevated. It's extreme. Starting this young, with his genetics, he's playing with fire."

Her words settled into me like lead. We weren't just fighting Daddy's disease. We were fighting our bloodline.

Uncle Mike squeezed my shoulder. "We pray this scared him straight. And if it didn't, we deal with it before he ends up like Bob."

The ride home was heavy with silence. Leo sniffled in the backseat, pale and wrecked from vomiting, whispering promises never to do it again. But I saw something in his eyes that scared me more than anything: not just shame, but curiosity. He'd tasted the quiet that alcohol offered, the numbing of guilt and fear, and once you learn that trick, it's hard to forget it.

"Are you going to tell Mom?" he asked when we pulled into the apartment complex.

"I have to."

"She's going to be so disappointed."

When we walked into the apartment, Mom was at the kitchen table folding laundry. She looked up and gave us that automatic smile she always wore after weekends with Daddy. The one that hoped for good news but braced for the worst.

"How was your weekend?" she asked, then froze. Her eyes landed on Leo. His pale skin, rumpled clothes, the way he avoided her gaze.

"Mom," I said quietly. "We need to talk."

The dish towel slipped from her hands. "What happened? Is Bob—"

"It's not Daddy," I said. "It's Leo."

Her eyes locked on him, and I saw her expression change as she pieced it together. The pallor, the slight sway in his stance, the smell of beer and vomit clinging to him even after we'd tried to clean him up.

"Oh no," she whispered. "Oh, Leo. No."

"Mom, I'm sorry—" Leo started, but she cut him off with a raised hand.

"How much did you drink?" Her voice stayed calm, but her hands trembled.

"Not that much. Just a couple of beers. I wanted to see—"

"You're twelve years old!" Her words cracked like a whip, the control she'd been clinging to snapping in an instant. "Twelve! You should be worried about homework and video games—not drowning yourself in alcohol!"

Leo flinched. "I just wanted to understand why Daddy—"

"I don't care why!" She was crying now, her voice shaking with rage and grief. "Do you know what it's like to watch your husband drink himself to death? To lie awake every night wondering if he'll come home alive? To explain to neighbors, teachers, and doctors why your family is falling apart?"

She pressed her hands to her face, words muffled. "I buried my marriage to alcoholism. I lost my home, my security, my hope for the future. I work double shifts until my feet bleed just to keep us fed. And now my twelve-year-old baby is passing out drunk in his father's house?"

Leo broke. Sobbing so hard his shoulders shook. "Mom, I'm sorry. I won't do it again, I promise—"

"That's what your father said!" she screamed. "Every single time. 'I'm sorry, Linda. I won't do it again, Linda. Just one more chance, Linda.' And I believed him. Over and over, I believed him."

Her body crumpled into the chair, voice breaking. "I can't do this again. I can't watch someone I love vanish into a bottle. I can't hold another family together while addiction tears it apart."

The apartment went still, only the sound of her crying and Leo's ragged breaths filling the room.

"Mom," Leo said in the smallest voice I'd ever heard, "I didn't mean to hurt you."

She looked at him then, eyes red and raw, and I saw fear replace her anger.

"Leo," she whispered, "do you understand what alcohol does to people like us? To brains like yours? Like your father's? It's not just a drink. It's poison. It's what turns fathers into strangers."

She went to him, kneeled so they were eye level. Her voice broke as she spoke. "I already lost your father to this disease. I will not lose you too. I can't. It would kill me, Leo."

Leo threw his arms around her neck, both of them sobbing, and I stood there watching. Watching my family fall apart and cling together all at once.

"I'm scared, Mommy," Leo whispered, using the word he hadn't in years. "I'm scared I'll turn into him."

"Then don't," she said fiercely, holding him as if she could keep him from slipping away. "Please, baby. Don't."

Later that night, lying awake while Leo tossed in his bed across the room, I stared at the ceiling and felt something harden inside me. He was twelve, and the cycle was already trying to pull him under.

My twelve-year-old brother had gotten drunk trying to understand why our father couldn't stop. He'd passed out in the same recliner where we'd found Daddy a hundred times.He'd learned that beer could make the noise in his head go quiet, even just for a little while.

And I'd watched it happen. At fourteen, I was watching the sickness slide from one Parker to the next, like it was hiding in our blood, waiting for its turn. I felt it circling Leo, pulling him toward the same emptiness that had swallowed Daddy.

I wanted to save him. But how do you save someone from something you can't even see? How do you tell a twelve-year-old that the thing that makes him feel calmer is the very thing that will ruin him? How do you fight against a disease that already lives inside our house, in our name, in our history?

I didn't know. I just knew I couldn't drink. I couldn't risk it. Because if Leo got lost and I got lost too, then who would be left to help Mommy? Who would keep us tethered to the idea of normal families, the kind who laughed at dinner tables instead of whispering over empty bottles?

That night, lying in my narrow bed while Leo breathed unevenly across the room, I reached for Grandpa's compass. The brass was cold at first, then warm as I rubbed my thumb along the smooth edge. I opened it slowly, watching the little needle steady itself on north. Always north, no matter how much the world around me spun.

The compass needle glowed faintly in the dim light from the window, pointing north toward something better than weekends in houses that smelled like rot and ash. Toward a world where families stayed whole, where fathers didn't forget their children, where kids didn't have to drink to breathe through the sadness.

Outside our window, I heard normal life: cars on the road, a dog barking, a neighbor's TV humming through the walls. Little reminders that the world still had ordinary in it, even if ours didn't.

I closed the compass and slid it back onto my nightstand, then pulled the blankets up to my chin.

I just listened to him breathe and prayed it wasn't too late. I prayed that love could be stronger than blood.

Chapter Eight

The College Mission

The walls of my bedroom looked less like walls and more like a map of exits. College brochures taped edge to edge, glossy doors to anywhere but here: Ohio State, Case Western, Cincinnati, Miami. Smiling kids sprawled on lawns, laughing in clean dorm rooms, walking across campuses that looked like little cities of possibility.

To me, they weren't just schools; they were lifelines.

At sixteen, every spare second I wasn't stocking shelves at Morrison's Grocery or juggling whatever new crisis cropped up at home, I was buried in SAT prep books, scholarship applications, and practice essays. It felt like my whole life depended on getting out, and maybe it did.

"You're working too hard, Olivia," Mommy said one night, finding me hunched over the kitchen table at midnight, papers spread across the surface like war maps.

"I have to," I muttered, circling yet another vocabulary word. "College isn't optional."

"You're up until three, you're working weekends, you've loaded your schedule with every AP class the school offers—"

"Because that's what it takes."

What I didn't tell her was that studying was the only time my brain went quiet. If I focused hard enough on verb conjugations and calculus proofs, I didn't have to think about Leo. I didn't have to think about my fourteen-year-old brother drinking more during weekends with Daddy, starting to walk and talk like him in ways that made me sick to my stomach.

The library became my refuge, not just for homework, but for research. Building a vision of who I wanted to become.

I devoured business magazines: *Fortune, Forbes, Bloomberg Businessweek.* I studied successful executives like they were textbook problems I could solve. If I could just figure out the formula (the right school, the right internships, the right path), I could become someone powerful enough that my past wouldn't matter.

That's when I found Margaret Carrington.

The article was in *Fortune*. "The Media Mogul Nobody Saw Coming." A photo showed a woman in her fifties, perfectly styled, standing in front of floor-to-ceiling windows overlooking Chicago. CEO of Carrington Media Group. She built a regional media empire that stretched across six states.

But it was the quote beneath her photo that stopped me cold.

"Success doesn't come from where you start. It comes from refusing to let your past define your future."

I read the whole profile. Twice. Margaret had grown up in a small Midwestern town, with parents who worked hard but never had much. She'd started at a tiny local news station, worked brutal hours, and clawed her way up. Now she ran a billion-dollar company.

Proof that girls from nowhere could become someone.

I tore out the page carefully, folded it, and tucked it into my scholarship application folder alongside my essay drafts and recommendation letters.

Someday I'd be like her: powerful, untouchable, so far from Millfield that no one would remember where I came from.

Mom wanted me to be sixteen in the ways she thought sixteen should look.

"You should be at football games. You should be going to parties, laughing with your friends. Not just studying."

"I don't want parties," I said. "I want Ohio State."

And I meant it. Columbus was far enough, two hours away, that I couldn't spend every weekend managing chaos. But not so far that people would accuse me of abandoning the family completely.

"What about Alex?" she asked. "You've been seeing him for six months. You never bring him around, and you never sound excited when he calls."

Alex Edmund. My first boyfriend, technically. Captain of the debate team, Princeton-bound, safe in all the ways I needed him to be. He was smart. He was predictable. He asked about homework and current events, not family secrets.

"Alex and I aren't... serious."

"Why not? He seems like a good boy. He cares about you."

I thought about yesterday in the library. I'd been crying over a B+ on a history exam, crying because I couldn't afford imperfection, and Alex sat across from me, watching.

"Is this really about the grade?" he asked gently. "Or is something else going on?"

I froze. He looked at me like he could see past the grades, past the perfect smile I practiced, all the way to the mess I didn't talk about.

"It's just the grade," I lied, shoving books into my bag.

"One test won't ruin your future."

"You don't understand."

"Then help me understand."

But I couldn't. I couldn't hand him the truth about Leo or Daddy or the way weekends felt like rehearsals for funerals. So I told him there was nothing to talk about and walked away. He looked hurt, but he didn't stop me. He never did.

Mommy was right. It wasn't a relationship. It was a study partnership. Safe, structured, shallow. Which was all I had space for anyway.

The SAT disaster hit on a gray Saturday in March.

I'd been preparing for six months: flashcards, tutors, practice tests. My score had to be flawless. Scholarships depended on it, and scholarships were the only way out.

Thirty minutes into the math section, I felt calm, almost powerful. And then my phone buzzed in my backpack. Once. Twice. Again. And again.

The proctor's warning replayed in my head: any use of electronic devices results in automatic disqualification.

I tried to ignore it. Tried to keep my eyes on the test. But in my family, a phone ringing that many times in a row only meant one thing: emergency.

By the time I finished the math section, my hands wouldn't stop shaking. I wasn't thinking about equations anymore. I was thinking about what disaster might be unfolding while I was locked in that silent room with a bubble sheet and a number two pencil.

During the break, I ran for my phone. Seven missed calls. All from Uncle Mike.

Seven calls in forty-five minutes.

My stomach dropped. I called him back, standing outside the school while kids munched on granola bars and compared test questions as if this was just another Saturday.

"Olivia? Thank God. Where were you?"

"I was taking the SATs. What happened?"

"It's your dad. His neighbor found him unconscious in the driveway. Looks like he fell trying to get in his car. Hit his head on the concrete. There's blood everywhere."

The world tilted sideways. I grabbed the brick wall to keep from falling.

"Is he... alive?"

"He's alive. Awake now. But, Olivia, he was drunk. Drunk enough that if he'd made it to the road, he could've killed himself or someone else."

"Where is he?"

"Emergency room."

"I'll come right now."

"No. Finish your test. There's nothing you can do that we can't handle."

"But—"

"Listen to me. Your SATs matter more than another one of Bob's crises. Don't let him drag your future down with him."

The call ended. I stood outside the school, shaking, staring at the doors. Other kids were going back in, chatting about spring break and AP classes, while I was stuck with the choice between saving my score or sitting in another waiting room while my father bled from his own chaos.

I went back inside.

But the words blurred on the page. The passages ran together. My mind kept skipping to Cleveland Metro, to blood on the driveway, to the thought of what if this was the last time. What if he died while I was bubbling in the wrong vocabulary answer?

I finished, but my brain had left long before the section did.

Alex was waiting by my locker with coffee and a look that made me want to bolt.

"How was it?" he asked.

"Terrible. A disaster."

"You always say that. You probably did better than you think."

"Alex…"

He lowered his voice. "I saw you on the phone outside. You looked terrified. What happened?"

For a second, I almost told him. About Uncle Mike, about Daddy, about the impossible choice I'd just made between test scores and family collapse. He would've listened. He would've cared.

But telling him meant pulling back the curtain on everything I'd worked so hard to keep hidden: the chaos, the shame, the real story behind why I worked myself to death for grades.

"It was nothing. Family stuff."

"Family stuff that shook you like that?"

"I said it was nothing."

He studied me for a long moment. "We've been together six months, and I don't think I know you at all. I know you're smart, disciplined, driven. But I don't know what you're afraid of, or what makes you happy, or why you never let me see you when you're not perfect."

"I'm not perfect—"

"You try to be. Every conversation we have is about school. When's the last time you told me something real?"

The truth sat in my throat, but I swallowed it. "I don't really do personal."

"Why not?"

"Because personal is messy. And I don't have time for messy."

He shook his head, almost sadly. "Messy is human, Olivia. That's what makes relationships real."

"I don't want real. I want functional."

"What does that even mean?"

"It means I want someone who understands that success matters more than feelings."

"That's not a relationship. That's a contract." His voice softened. "And the fact that you can't trust me with what's really going on tells me everything I need to know."

I wanted to stop him. I wanted to explain. But he was already walking away, leaving me with a cup of coffee I couldn't drink and the sinking realization that he was right.

He'd been dating the version of me that was safe. The polished, perfect one with the carefully managed smile. Not the girl whose father was bleeding in a hospital bed.

And I couldn't decide if losing him hurt more than keeping the secret.

I found Leo in the garage that Sunday evening. Uncle Mike was supposed to be there soon to drive us back, but Leo wasn't packing his bag. He was sitting on an upside-down bucket, a Budweiser in his hand as if it belonged there. His face tilted back, throat working slowly as he swallowed. Three empty bottles sat neatly at his feet like soldiers standing guard.

"Leo?" My voice echoed in the cold garage. The smell of gasoline and stale beer mixed together, sharp in my nose.

He looked up, eyes glassy but steady. Not wild, not sloppy. Just... dulled. "Hey, Livvy. Just taking a break from all the family drama."

My stomach tightened. "How long have you been drinking?"

"Just started." He waved one hand lazily, but I saw the empties lined up. "Don't look at me like that."

"Like what?"

"Like I'm turning into him." He tilted his head toward the house, where Daddy had been passed out since Friday night, the sound of his snores carrying faintly through the walls. "This isn't the same."

But it was. I knew it in my gut.

"Leo, you promised," I said. "After the hospital. You swore you wouldn't drink again."

"I promised I wouldn't drink to figure him out. I never said I wouldn't use it to deal with all this." His hand made a tired sweep at the whole garage, at the world we were stuck in.

His words chilled me. He sounded just like Daddy, drawing thin lines between choice and need.

"How often?" I asked, my throat dry.

"Not much. Just weekends here, when it gets too heavy. Just when I need the noise to quiet down for a while."

"That's exactly how it starts," I whispered. "That's exactly how it started with him."

"I can handle it." He lifted the bottle and sipped slowly, careful. "There's a difference between choosing it and needing it."

But I could hear Daddy's voice in those words. Different decade, same excuses.

"Remember the ER?" I pressed. "The doctor's face when they said you could've died? You think this is different, but it's not."

"I'm not drinking to pass out anymore." His tone sharpened, defensive. "I'm drinking to survive. To make this bearable."

"Leo—"

"You don't know what it's like." His voice cracked, loud enough to bounce off the garage walls. "You're already half gone, Livvy. You bury yourself in your AP classes and SAT prep and pretend none of this matters. You've stopped feeling. You've stopped caring."

"That's not true."

"Isn't it? When's the last time you cried about him? When's the last time his drinking kept you awake at night? You've turned yourself into a robot. I can't do that."

"So you're going to drink instead?" My voice came out sharper than I intended, but I was terrified. Not just because he was drinking, but because he was drinking with purpose.

"I'm choosing to survive," he said again, quieter this time. "Same as you. Your drug is grades. Mine's a few beers. At least I'm honest about it."

From inside the house, Uncle Mike's voice cut through the quiet: "Kids! Time to go!"

Leo stood, too steady for someone who'd downed that much. He popped a piece of gum, chewed quickly, then splashed water from a bottle onto his face and hands.

"You're not going to tell him," he said, eyes locked on mine.

"Leo—"

"If you do, they'll eventually end visits. Dad needs someone. He needs to know someone still believes in him."

"Drinking during visits isn't caring. It's killing yourself right alongside him."

"Maybe." He grabbed his backpack, shoulders stiff. "But it's the only way I can stand watching him choose alcohol over us every single weekend."

We stood there, staring at each other across the concrete floor. Fourteen and sixteen, already carrying the weight of choices far bigger than us. His armor was beer. Mine was grades. Both working, both breaking us at the same time.

"You coming?" Uncle Mike shouted again.

"Coming!" Leo yelled back. He gave me one last look. "This never happened, Livvy. Not to Uncle Mike. Not to Mom. Not to anyone."

"What if it destroys you?" I whispered.

"Then at least I'll go down fighting for him," he said, voice hard. "Not running away to college and pretending none of this matters."

He walked past me, smelling of beer and mint gum, leaving me in the garage with the bottles lined up like proof of where this was headed.

The envelope was thick. The kind that mattered. I pulled it from the mailbox, my hands already shaking. Ohio State. I ripped it open right there in the hall, heart pounding so hard I thought it might jump out of my chest.

Congratulations. Honors program. Accepted. The words blurred as my eyes filled with tears. This was it. The escape I'd been building since middle school. Every sleepless night. Every extra credit assignment. Every Saturday bagging groceries. Proof that I could make it out.

But then the numbers. Tuition: twenty-four thousand a year. Room and board: twelve. Books and expenses: three more. Even with the partial scholarship of eight thousand annually, I'd still need over thirty grand. For one year.

The acceptance letter nearly slipped from my hand. Thirty thousand dollars. Where was I supposed to find that?

The letters on the page turned into prison bars. Ohio State might as well have been Mars.

That night I lay in bed with the Ohio State letter in my hands, staring at the words until they stopped making sense. Honors Program. Partial scholarship. Everything I'd worked toward for years, yet still not enough to make it real.

It should have felt like freedom. Instead, it felt like I was being asked to gamble my future on one interview. Win the full ride, and I could escape. Lose it, and I'd be chained here by debt or family obligation.

"What are you gonna do?" Leo asked from across the room, his voice muffled by the pillow.

"I don't know. I got into Ohio State, but I need the full scholarship to actually go."

He was quiet for a moment before asking, "When's the interview?"

"March fifteenth."

"Daddy's getting worse," he said, his voice low. "Every weekend he looks sicker. Like he's disappearing."

"I know."

"Maybe if you stayed... maybe if he knew you were still around, he wouldn't give up. And you wouldn't have to worry about money."

"Leo, staying here won't cure him. It'll just trap me with him."

"But what if he dies while you're gone? What if something happens and you're not here? And what if you don't get the scholarship anyway?"

His words landed heavily in my stomach. What if he was right? What if I went away and Daddy died while I was chasing my dreams? What if I failed the interview and ended up stuck here anyway? Would I carry that guilt forever?

"I don't know," I whispered.

I could hear Leo's breathing in the dark. Not asleep, just pretending. Probably asking himself the same impossible questions. Was family supposed to mean staying no matter what? Or did love sometimes mean leaving?

On my nightstand, the acceptance letter sat right beside it. The letter promising a way out if I could just win one more competition.

"Livvy?" Leo's voice was so soft I almost missed it.

"Yeah?"

"Are you really gonna try for the scholarship?"

I thought about lying. But he deserved better than that.

"I think so. I have to."

"Even if Daddy gets worse?"

"Even then."

Silence stretched out before he said, in a voice that suddenly sounded older, "I get it. I don't want you to go, but I get it. You're not like us. You're the one who's gonna make it out."

"You could too," I said quickly. "You could get your GED, go to community college—"

"No." He sounded certain. "I'm too much like Daddy. We both know it."

I wanted to argue, but the words stuck. Because some part of me, the part I didn't want to admit, was afraid he was right.

"But that's okay," Leo went on. "Maybe you leaving is enough. Maybe that's how things get better."

"What if I don't get the scholarship?" I asked. "What if I mess up the interview?"

"Then you'll figure something else out. You don't quit, Livvy."

"What if something happens to you while I'm gone?"

"Then you'll come home for my funeral and give a really good speech about how I was too stubborn to let you save me."

"Leo, that's not funny."

"It's a little funny."

I wanted to cry, but I was too tired. Too worn down by years of chaos and guilt. Instead, I just listened to his voice.

"Hey, Livvy?"

"Yeah?"

"When you're at Ohio State, will you send me pictures? Of your dorm. The campus. Stuff like that."

"If I get the scholarship and make it there, I'll send you pictures. I promise."

"And maybe come home sometimes? Christmas, Easter?"

"I'll be home for breaks. I promise."

"Okay." His voice softened, fading as he turned over. "That sounds good."

He drifted off, and I lay awake another hour, holding the letter, trying to picture Columbus. Huge libraries bigger than our whole apartment. Dining halls with clean tables. Friends who only worried about exams or parties, not hospital visits and pawn shops. It sounded lonely. It also sounded like freedom.

Tomorrow I'd start preparing for the interview. Researching the committee. Practicing answers. Fighting for the chance to leave.

I thought about the Margaret Carrington article I'd torn from *Fortune* last week, the one now tucked in my scholarship folder. She'd grown up in a small Midwestern town, just like me: parents who worked hard but never had much. Now, she ran a billion-dollar media empire from a Chicago office with floor-to-ceiling windows.

"Success doesn't come from where you start," she'd said in the interview. *"It comes from refusing to let your past define your future."*

She'd chosen herself, left her small town behind, and built something powerful enough that no one remembered where she came from anymore.

That's what I wanted. Not just college. Not just escape. But the kind of success that completely erased your origin story.

Maybe that's what the scholarship committee needed to hear: not that I was running away, but that I was running toward something. Toward the person Margaret Carrington had become.

Someone who'd proven that girls from nowhere could make it.

I went back online that night, pulling up everything I could find about Margaret Carrington. Most articles repeated the same story: small-town girl makes good, building an empire from nothing.

But one older piece caught my attention: a *Chicago Tribune* profile from 2007 that mentioned her husband, David Carrington, and their business empire. The timeline felt strange. There was a gap of three years in the early 2000s during which Margaret seemed to vanish from public records. The article didn't explain it; it just said she "rebuilt her portfolio with strategic acquisitions during a transition period."

What kind of transition makes someone disappear for three years?

Another piece mentioned her entertainment division: "Carrington Media's portfolio includes seven upscale venues across the Midwest." Nightclubs. I skimmed past it; nightclubs seemed boring compared to media empires.

Who cared about bars and dance floors when you could own television stations?

I bookmarked the articles anyway and printed the best ones for my interview prep folder. If they asked me about successful businesswomen, I'd have Margaret Carrington ready, every detail memorized.

But that night, I fell asleep with Leo's words in my head: *Maybe you leaving is how our family gets better.*

Maybe he was right. Maybe sometimes you had to save yourself first, even if it felt cruel. Maybe north wasn't pointing away from my family; it was pointing toward the person I had to become.

Margaret Carrington had done exactly that, and she had built an empire.

Or maybe I was simply trying to convince myself that leaving was noble rather than selfish.

Either way, the needle remained steady. And for the first time, I was prepared to follow it if I could persuade a room full of strangers that I was worth the chance.

Chapter Nine

Leo's Descent

SPRING 2010

The call came at eleven-thirty on a Friday night. I was hunched over my Ohio State application essay, trying to polish sentences until they gleamed. Mommy had already collapsed into bed after another double shift at the diner. The phone rang sharp and loud, the sound of trouble.

"Is this Linda Parker?" The voice was official, clipped.

"This is her daughter. What's wrong?"

"This is Officer Williams with Millfield Police. We have your brother Leo in custody."

My heart sank. "For what?"

"Public intoxication, underage drinking, and possession of marijuana. He was arrested at the homecoming dance."

I dropped into a kitchen chair, my essay forgotten. "Is he okay? Is he hurt?"

"He's fine physically. But he needs to be picked up from juvenile detention. We've been calling your mother for two hours."

"She's asleep. She works nights. I'll wake her up."

I hung up and sat for a beat in the quiet kitchen. Leo hadn't just been drinking at Dad's anymore. He'd carried it into school, into public, where the consequences weren't just hangovers but court dates.

I shook Mommy awake. "Mommy, there's an emergency."

Her eyes flew open instantly, fear etched into her face. She'd trained for midnight crisis calls after years of living with Bob Parker.

"What is it? Is it your father?"

"It's Leo. He's been arrested."

The Millfield Police Department looked like what it was: a place designed to deal with barking dogs and traffic tickets, not the implosion of a family.

Leo was slumped in a plastic chair in the juvenile holding area, still in his homecoming clothes but looking like a stranger. His shirt was wrinkled, his hair a mess, his eyes glassy and unfocused in the way I knew too well.

But instead of looking defeated, he couldn't stop moving. His leg bounced. His fingers tapped. He picked at the skin on his hands until it bled. When we walked in, he turned away like the blank wall was suddenly fascinating.

"Leo," Mommy whispered, as if he might spook if she spoke too loudly.

"I'm sorry, Mom. I'm so sorry." But he still wouldn't look at her. Words tumbled out fast, like he had to outrun the truth. "I didn't mean for it to get this bad. Sarah had a flask. Trevor had weed. It was homecoming; everyone was celebrating. I thought I could handle it. I thought I was being careful."

His voice had that frantic edge, the same one I'd heard a thousand times from Dad. Desperate to make reckless behavior sound logical.

"How much did you drink?" Mommy asked.

"Not that much. Four or five shots and a couple of beers. All before the dance. But I wasn't that drunk. I was just relaxed." His leg bounced faster, shredding a tissue he'd found. "The cops just wanted to pick on me. Everyone else was drinking too."

Four or five shots. A couple of beers. For a kid his size, that was enough to land him in the ER.

"Leo, that's not 'not that much,'" I said. "That's dangerous."

"I was fine. Totally in control. The cops just picked on me because I was having fun."

The denial was textbook Bob Parker. The same shrugging off, the same blame-shifting, the same refusal to acknowledge reality that had defined our father's life.

"Mr. Parker was found unconscious in the school parking lot," Officer Williams told Mommy, her voice clipped and professional. "A student thought he was having a medical emergency and called 911. When paramedics arrived, he was intoxicated and in possession of marijuana."

"Unconscious?" Mommy whispered.

"He'd passed out next to a car. Could've been there for hours if someone hadn't found him."

I watched Mommy's face as the words landed. Leo hadn't just been drinking at the dance. He'd been drinking until his body gave out. Passed out in a dark parking lot, vulnerable in every way a fifteen-year-old shouldn't be.

"The marijuana possession adds another charge," Officer Williams continued. "He'll need to appear in family court Monday morning."

"Family court," Mommy repeated, her voice flat with disbelief.

"Judge Warren. Nine a.m. Don't be late."

On the ride home, I sat in the back seat while Mommy drove in silence. Uncle Mike stared out the window.

"Where's he even getting the alcohol?" I finally asked. "He's fifteen. Someone has to be buying it for him."

Uncle Mike sighed. "Same places kids always do. Older friends. Fake IDs that nobody checks. There's that new place over in the warehouse district. Club something. Vertical, I think."

"They serve fifteen-year-olds?"

"They don't card properly. Cops know about it, but it's connected somehow. Protected."

"Protected by who?"

Uncle Mike's jaw tightened. "By money, Olivia. By people who can make problems disappear. That's how it works when you've got real power."

I thought about that. About how some people could break all the rules and never face consequences. While kids like Leo got arrested for doing exactly what those clubs encouraged.

Money made you untouchable. Money bought protection.

That's what I needed. Not just enough to get out. Enough to never be powerless again.

Monday morning, I sat in Millfield Family Court and watched my little brother shuffle into the courtroom in an orange jumpsuit that swallowed him whole. He was shackled at the wrists, his shoulders hunched, his eyes darting nervously.

He looked exactly like Daddy had during his DUI hearings. Same jumpsuit. Same courtroom. Same shame mixed with a spark of defiance. It was like watching our family history fast-forwarded onto Leo's body.

"Leo Parker," Judge Warren said, scanning the file in front of her. "You're charged with underage drinking, public intoxication, and possession of marijuana. How do you plead?"

"Guilty, Your Honor," his lawyer answered before Leo could open his mouth.

The judge studied him. "This is your first arrest, but the record notes previous police interactions related to alcohol. Care to explain?"

Leo's eyes flicked toward us: Mommy with her hands pressed together like she was praying, Uncle Mike shaking his head, me trying to look supportive even though inside I was furious.

"I've had some problems with drinking," Leo admitted quietly. "But I'm working on it."

"Working on it how?"

"I'm... trying to cut back. Only drinking on weekends. Only when the stress gets really bad."

Judge Warren gave him the kind of look people give when they've heard the same excuse a hundred times.

"Mr. Parker, you're fifteen. There should be no stress in your life that requires alcohol. And 'cutting back' isn't the answer. The law requires abstinence."

"Yes, Your Honor."

She laid out the sentence: forty hours of community service, weekly substance abuse counseling, random drug and alcohol testing for six months. Violate anything, and juvenile detention would be waiting.

Leo nodded, but I could see it in his eyes. He was already calculating. Already figuring out how to appear compliant while still sneaking drinks. Exactly the way Daddy had gamed the system for years.

"And I'm recommending family therapy," Judge Warren added. "Addiction is a family disease. Recovery is more successful with support from everyone."

Family therapy started the next Wednesday in a room that smelled like vanilla candles and looked too cozy for the conversations happening inside it. Dr. Collins had kind eyes and calm patience that made me believe she'd heard everything before.

She asked to speak with us one at a time, then together. By the third session, she turned to Leo.

"Why do you drink?"

He slouched in his chair. "I don't know."

"You don't know?"

"I mean... everything sucks, I guess." He started pulling at a loose thread on the chair.

"Be more specific. What sucks?"

"Stuff." His eyes went to the ceiling, jaw tight, signaling he was done cooperating.

"Leo, what happens when you don't drink?"

"Nothing. Same crap, different day."

"And when you do drink?"

His eyes flicked toward her, then away again. "Things get quieter."

"Quieter how?"

He shifted in his seat. "Like someone turned down the volume."

Dr. Collins scribbled something down. "What kind of volume? Outside noise, or inside your head?"

"Both. Neither. I don't know." His voice sharpened. "Why does it matter?"

"I'm trying to understand what you feel when—"

"I don't feel anything when I drink. That's the point." His words cracked like a whip. "Everyone wants me to feel. Talk about my feelings. Process them. Sometimes I just want to stop feeling for a while. Is that illegal?"

"It's not illegal to want relief," Dr. Collins said gently. "But alcohol isn't—"

"Yeah, yeah, I know the speech. Not safe. Not healthy. I've heard it all."

His voice rose, his eyes suddenly blazing. "You know what's really unsafe? Living in this house. Watching my dad drink himself to death while everyone pretends we're gonna be fine."

"That sounds terrifying," she said softly.

"Don't." His voice broke. "Don't repeat it back like you get it."

"You're right. I don't know what it's like to be you."

Leo went quiet. His fingers worried that thread again. Then his voice dropped to almost nothing. "It's like those dreams where you're trying to scream but no sound comes out. That's what being sober feels like now. Like I'm drowning, and nobody can hear me."

Dr. Collins leaned forward, her voice gentle. "And drinking changes that?"

Leo froze. His face went blank like he realized he'd let something slip. "I guess."

"Can you tell me more about that drowning feeling?"

"No." The word was sharp, final. "I can't, actually. Because every time I try, adults start preaching. Healthy coping strategies, family meetings, journaling. All the stuff that doesn't work."

"What doesn't work about it?"

"All of it!" His voice cracked, the composure he'd been clinging to finally giving way.

"You want me to journal? My dad is drinking himself to death. You want me to practice deep breathing? My sister's planning her escape route. You want me to talk to Mom about my feelings? She's too busy working double shifts so we're not homeless."

Tears slipped out then. Angry, hot tears that he wiped with the back of his sleeve like he was furious at himself for letting anyone see.

"So yeah," he said, his voice shaking, "sometimes I drink. Sometimes I just want my brain to shut up for a while. Sometimes I want to stop thinking about how everything is falling apart."

"Leo," I said quietly, "drinking isn't going to fix any of it."

His head whipped toward me. His face was red, wet, and burning with fury. "Neither is your perfect GPA, Olivia. At least I'm not pretending my coping mechanism is healthy."

The words landed like a slap. "What's that supposed to mean?"

"It means you've turned yourself into some kind of academic robot so you don't have to feel anything. You're so busy

planning your big escape that you've checked out completely."

"That's not true—"

"When's the last time you cried about Dad? When's the last time you stayed up worrying about what happens to us after you leave?"

I opened my mouth, but nothing came. Because he was right. And he knew it. And I knew it.

"See?" Leo's voice was hollow now, empty of fight. "At least when I'm drunk, I admit I'm running away. You call it ambition. You call it achievement. But really? We're both just trying to survive this family without drowning in it."

"Kids," Dr. Collins cut in softly, "can we shift to talking about what you each need from one another?"

But Leo was already on his feet, swiping at his face with the back of his hand.

"I need everyone to stop pretending this can be fixed," he said. "I need people to stop asking why I drink when the answer's right in front of us. And I need my sister to stop looking at me like I'm already Dad just because I found a way to cope that doesn't get me gold stars."

He walked to the door, then stopped with his hand on the handle.

"You want to know the difference between me and Dad?" His voice was flat, steady now. "I know this isn't sustainable. I know I can't drink every time life gets hard. But I also know pretending everything's fine while the whole family falls apart isn't sustainable either."

"Leo, wait—" Mommy's voice cracked.

"I'll be in the car," he said, and left.

The session ended with Dr. Collins assigning us all "healthy coping strategies" and promising follow-ups. But on the ride home in Uncle Mike's car, the only thing I could feel was the weight of what had just happened.

Leo wasn't experimenting anymore. He wasn't sneaking drinks out of curiosity or rebellion. He was medicating. He was fifteen years old and already dosing himself against pain too big for a kid to hold.

And the worst part was, maybe he understood that truth better than any of us wanted to admit.

Two weeks later, the bottom dropped again.

Leo got expelled.

Not for the homecoming mess. That had only landed him with a suspension and counseling he sat through with a scowl.

This time, he showed up to first-period American History drunk.

"I wasn't that drunk," he told us as we sat in the principal's office. "Just a couple of shots of vodka in my orange juice. I was perfectly fine."

"Fine enough that Mrs. Thompson could smell it on you from across the room?" I asked.

"She hates me. She's been looking for an excuse since the arrest."

But I could see the truth in his pupils, wide and glassy, in the way his body swayed just slightly even in a chair. This wasn't a "couple of shots." This was enough to be obvious at eight in the morning. Either he was still drunk from the night before, or he'd been drinking heavily before school. Both were worse than anything we'd faced yet.

"Zero tolerance," Principal Andrews said to Mommy in that weary voice of his. "Any student under the influence is expelled. That's the rule."

"What about an alternative program? Counseling? Something that lets him finish?"

"Mrs. Parker, your son walked into school drunk at eight a.m. That's not a mistake. It's addiction. And our school isn't equipped to handle that."

And just like that, Leo's future at Millfield High was over. No diploma. No path to the kind of achievement that might have saved him from Daddy's shadow.

At fifteen, all he had left were GED programs and maybe a trade school if he could ever get sober long enough to follow through.

"I'm sorry," he said in the car, though it didn't sound like an apology. More like resignation. "I know you wanted me to graduate with my class."

Mommy's voice cracked as she fought back tears. "I wanted you to have choices, Leo. Choices that didn't look like this."

"I still have choices."

"Like what?"

"GED. A trade. Something besides sitting in classrooms eight hours a day pretending to care about the Revolutionary War while my family wages one of its own."

"Or you could get sober and get your life back," I said.

He looked at me, his face tight. "My life was never on track, Livvy. That's the difference. You were born knowing how to function. I was born broken, like Dad."

"You weren't born broken," I snapped. "You're breaking yourself."

He gave a tired half-smile. "Maybe. Or maybe I'm just being honest about who I am. You're the one pretending you can achieve your way out of Parker family genetics."

Despite everything (the arrest, the expulsion, the drinking that wasn't even a secret anymore), Leo still sat with me while I practiced my valedictorian speech.

It was a Tuesday night in November, two weeks before I'd stand at that podium and say goodbye to high school. I was pacing our cramped living room with index cards in my hand. Leo was on the couch, Rex tucked under his arm like he was still a little kid. But I could smell the beer on his breath from where I stood.

"'Today we stand at the threshold of unlimited possibility,'" I read out loud, trying to sound inspired even though the words felt fake with my brother drinking ten feet away. "'We are the generation that will solve tomorrow's problems with today's determination.'"

"That's good," Leo said, his voice careful, too careful, like he was working not to slur. "Very inspirational. Very Olivia."

"What's that supposed to mean?" I asked, but really I was watching him, counting the signs. His posture, his timing, how many beers I guessed he'd had.

He smirked faintly. "It means you sound like someone on top of the mountain giving a speech to people who are still stuck in the valley."

He wasn't wrong. But it stung anyway. I worked for my spot on that mountain. Every sleepless night, every test, every shift at Morrison's Grocery. I earned it.

"I earned my place here," I snapped.

"I know. I'm just saying... your speech doesn't see the people buried under avalanches."

Even drunk, he was still smart. Still my brilliant little brother. And that was the part that made my chest ache. The way his mind was still there, fighting through the haze.

"Help me make it better, then," I said, sitting across from him.

"Sure." He leaned forward, suddenly focused like the old Leo who made teachers smile. But when he moved, the wave of beer smell hit me again, sharp and sour.

"But first," he grinned, and I braced myself, waiting for him to ask for money or slip out for another drink, "can you do Principal Andrews? You know, the way he does announcements?"

"Leo—"

"Come on, Livvy. Just once. You do it the best." His grin was crooked, the same one from when we were kids. But his eyes, glassy and tired, made it hurt to look at him.

I wanted to yell at him. I wanted to count his bottles and tell him he was killing himself. But instead, I cleared my throat and slipped into that nasal, self-important tone: "'Students of Millfield High School, please remember that chewing gum is not permitted in the hallways, as it creates an unsanitary environment that reflects poorly on our academic institution.'"

Leo burst into laughter, real laughter, the kind that filled our tiny apartment with warmth for a minute. And I laughed too, even though my stomach was tight with worry.

"That's perfect!" he said, still laughing. "Like he's announcing the cure for cancer when it's just gum."

For ten whole minutes, we giggled, doing voices of our teachers, falling into the kind of silly fun only siblings can have. And even as I laughed, I kept noticing his timing was a little off. And how often he glanced toward the kitchen, where more beer waited.

"You should be a comedian," I said when we finally caught our breath.

"Maybe I will. If the whole

high-school-dropout-with-a-criminal-record thing doesn't work out." His smile slipped.

"Leo—"

"I'm kidding. Mostly." He went quiet, staring at his hands. "You know I'm proud of you, right? For everything. Valedictorian, Ohio State, all of it."

"Even though I'm abandoning the family?"

"You're not abandoning us. You're surviving. I just..." His throat worked. "I wish I was strong enough to do the same."

"You are strong enough. You just have to choose sobriety instead of Daddy's path."

"What if I can't?" His voice was so small I barely heard it. "What if it's stronger than me?"

The air between us got heavy.

"Then you get help," I said. "Not court-ordered crap. Real treatment. Before it's too late."

"Like Dad? Like all those rehabs that never worked?"

"You're not him. You're younger. There's still time."

He was quiet for a long time, and I saw it on his face. That war between hope and the pull of another beer.

"Will you help me?" he asked finally. "If I decide to try. Will you help me figure it out?"

"Always," I said without hesitation.

"Even when you're at Ohio State? Even when you've got your new life?"

I froze for half a second, and he caught it. He always caught it. His face fell.

"Never mind," he said, his voice flat now. "I shouldn't have asked."

"Leo, it's not that. It's just—"

"You don't need to explain. I get it. You can't save me." He looked down at his lap. "I wasn't asking you to. I just wanted to know if you'd still be my sister when I mess up."

I reached across the table, my hand trembling. "I'll always be your sister."

"Will you?" He looked at me then, his eyes wet and glassy. "Or will you be the college girl who used to have a brother before he became just like Dad?"

That hurt in a way I can't even explain because I could see the fear behind Leo's words. He wasn't only scared of turning into Daddy. He was scared of me leaving him behind, the way I'd already left Daddy in my own way.

"I will always love you," I told him, and I meant it with everything I had.

"But you won't always stay."

"No," I admitted. "I won't always stay."

"Then I guess I need to figure out how to love you while you go, and how to love myself while I'm stuck here with everything you get to escape."

He stood up then. His legs weren't steady, but they held him, and I knew he was headed for another beer. The fragile connection we'd just made slipped away, replaced by the reality I couldn't fix.

"Leo—"

"Thanks for doing the impression," he said over his shoulder. "It helped. For a few minutes, it helped."

I sat in the living room with my stack of index cards, listening to the hiss of a beer can opening in the kitchen. Even our laughter was contaminated now. Every moment of joy with him carried the aftertaste of addiction. I couldn't just laugh anymore. I was always calculating how many beers he'd had, wondering how far gone he was. The same boy who made me laugh until my stomach hurt was now the same boy slurring words and following Daddy's path step for step.

And I was powerless to stop him.

Two weeks later, I stood at the podium in Millfield High's gym, looking out at three hundred graduates and their families, holding the speech Leo had once helped me revise.

Mommy sat in the third row, pride lighting up her face. Uncle Mike was beside her. Leo's seat was empty. Too hungover to show up for my graduation.

"Today we stand at the threshold of unlimited possibility," I began. "We are the generation that will choose triumph over tragedy, hope over despair."

The words rang out like I believed them. Parents nodded. Teachers smiled.

"As we move forward, we understand that sometimes the most courageous thing you can do is choose your own path, even when others need you to stay."

I saw Mommy's face shift slightly at that line. Uncle Mike squeezed her hand.

The gym thundered with applause. People stood, clapping and cheering like I'd just delivered something profound instead of a seventeen-year-old's attempt to dress survival up as courage.

But walking back to my seat, diploma in hand, I couldn't shake the thought: maybe there's no real difference between courage and selfishness. Maybe it just depends on who's telling the story.

In four months, I'd be in Columbus, to the life I'd been building since I was twelve. And Leo would still be here, drinking in Daddy's chair.

I'd made it sound like a victory instead of what it actually was: escape.

The confession came a week later, while Mommy stirred spaghetti in our tiny kitchen and I sat at the table with college forms spread around me.

"Olivia," she said softly, not looking up from the pot. "I need to tell you something about Leo."

"What about him?"

"I see your father in his eyes now."

The words dropped like stones, sending ripples I didn't want to face.

"What do you mean?"

"I mean I recognize it. The desperation mixed with defiance. The way his face changes when he talks about drinking. It's the same look your father had when the addiction fully took over."

"Leo's not Daddy," I said quickly. "He's just going through a rough phase."

Mommy turned, her voice sharp with the authority of someone who had lived this before. "Honey, I lived with your father's addiction for sixteen years. I know what it looks like when someone crosses from drinking to needing to drink. And Leo has crossed that line already."

I wanted to fight her. To insist he was still just a kid acting out. But deep down, I knew she was right. I'd watched the same shifts. The drinking that wasn't occasional anymore, the casual way he talked about it, the way it had become his solution for everything he didn't want to feel.

"What are we supposed to do?" I asked.

Her shoulders sagged. "I don't know. I tried everything with your father. Threats, ultimatums, therapy, treatment, love, anger, patience, boundaries. Nothing worked until he decided to recover, and by then it was too late for our marriage."

"It's not too late for Leo."

"Isn't it?" Her eyes were wet now, and her voice cracked. "He's fifteen. He's been arrested. He's been expelled. He's drinking every day. How much worse does it have to get before we admit love isn't enough?"

"We can't give up on him."

"I'm not giving up," she said, finally facing me with tears streaming down her cheeks. "I'm saying I can't save another Parker man from a disease that's determined to take them both."

Her grief was raw, not the hidden tears she used to cry in the bathroom, but open, broken grief for the son slipping away in front of her.

"I won't do it again, Olivia," she whispered. "I won't spend the next twenty years making excuses, enabling, pretending love can cure a brain disease."

"What does that mean?" I asked, even though I wasn't sure I wanted the answer.

"It means if Leo keeps choosing alcohol instead of recovery, he's choosing to lose his family too," Mommy said. Her voice was steady, but I could see her hands trembling. "Because I can't live with active addiction anymore. I don't have the strength to manage another addict's chaos."

"Mom—"

"I buried my marriage to alcoholism," she said quietly. "I won't bury my sanity to it too."

Two nights later, I came home from Morrison's Grocery and found Leo in the kitchen with Mommy's purse open on the counter.

"What are you doing?"

He jumped like he'd been shocked, then tried to close the purse and back away like nothing had happened.

"Nothing. Just looking for gum."

But the crumpled bills in his hand told the truth. Mommy's tip money. The cash that was supposed to cover groceries for the week.

"Leo, put the money back."

"What money?" He tried shoving it into his pocket, but his movements were sloppy, the kind of clumsy that comes with alcohol and desperation.

"The money you just took from Mom's purse."

"I didn't take anything. I borrowed twenty bucks. I'll pay it back."

I just stared at him. My fifteen-year-old brother. The same boy who used to build Lego cities on our living room floor, who used to hide behind me when Daddy got scary, who once trusted me to protect him from everything. Now he was stealing from the woman who worked herself raw just to keep us fed.

"Leo, do you even see Mom's hands?"

"What?"

"Her hands. The cuts from washing dishes, the burns from hot plates, the way they shake from carrying trays sixteen hours a day."

He blinked, a little lost in the haze, but I pressed on.

"She's killing herself for us. Literally working until her body breaks down. And you're stealing the money she earned serving coffee to truckers who treat her like trash."

"It's just twenty dollars—"

"It's not just twenty dollars! It's what she earned smiling at people who yell at her about cold food. It's what she made standing on her feet all day after already pulling a double shift yesterday. And you're taking it to buy poison."

His face started to crack, but I couldn't stop.

"You're stealing. Not borrowing. Stealing. We both know you'll never pay it back. We both know what it's for."

"I just need—"

"You need to stop destroying the only person in this family still holding us together!" My voice broke. "Mom already lost her husband to alcohol. She lost her home, her security, her marriage. And now you're forcing her to lose her son to the same thing."

"She's not losing me—"

"She is! Every day you're less Leo and more Bob. Less my brother and more another Parker man who steals from women who love him."

He clutched the bills, and for just a second, I saw it. A flicker of recognition. Not excuses. Not defiance. Just a flash of awareness about what he'd become.

"I don't know how to stop," he whispered.

"You start by putting that money back. You apologize when Mom gets home."

"And then what? Pretend I can handle all this sober?"

"Then you get help. Real help. Not the counseling you fake your way through. Treatment for the disease that's eating you alive."

"What if it doesn't work? What if I'm already too far gone?"

"You're fifteen, Leo. You're not too far gone for anything."

"Daddy started when he was my age."

"Daddy didn't have anyone who understood addiction. You do. You have people who can help you make a different choice."

His voice dropped so low I almost didn't hear it. "What if I don't want to choose differently? What if being like Daddy feels easier than trying to stay strong?"

And there it was. The truth beneath every excuse. He wasn't drinking to understand Dad or to rebel. He was drinking because it was easier to be numb than to be alive in our family.

"Then you'll die," I said flatly. "Not today. Not tomorrow. But eventually. And Mom will bury another Parker man who chose a bottle over the people who loved him."

"Maybe that'd be easier for everyone."

"Don't you dare." My voice turned sharp. "Don't you dare talk like that when Mom is breaking herself to keep us together."

"I'm not talking about killing myself," he muttered. "I'm talking about accepting who I am. Some people are just casualties of their genetics."

"You're not a casualty. You're a fifteen-year-old making choices that feel like solutions but are really symptoms."

He looked down at the money, then back at me. "I don't know how to want sobriety more than I want the noise to stop."

"Then figure it out. Because I can't watch you become him. I've spent my whole childhood protecting you. I won't spend my adulthood watching you drink yourself into the same grave."

"So you're giving up on me too?"

"I'm choosing my survival over saving someone who doesn't want to be saved."

He stared at me for a long time, and I saw it. The moment he realized I'd hit my limit. That the sister who always pulled him out of the fire wasn't going to this time.

"You're becoming a thief just like him," I said, my voice breaking with grief. "And I won't drown alongside you."

He walked to his room and closed the door quietly, and it felt final.

I stood there in the kitchen, staring at the purse on the counter. Mommy was out working herself to exhaustion at the diner. Daddy was drinking himself to death in a house that smelled like rot. Leo was following him step for step, beer for beer.

And me? I was clinging to school and college applications, pretending that escape could break the cycle.

But it didn't feel like escape. It felt like betrayal.

At seventeen, I was beginning to understand that sometimes love means standing by while the people you care about ruin themselves and choosing not to go down with them. That sometimes the most moral decision feels like betrayal. That growing up means facing the truth: you can't save people who don't want saving, not even when they're your own blood. Not even when they're your little brother.

And that was the hardest lesson of all.

Leo's addiction wasn't just costing him his health or his future. It was costing him me, too. It was teaching me that no amount of loyalty or love could conquer the pull of genetics and trauma. At seventeen, I was realizing that the choice that breaks your heart might be the only one that keeps you alive.

I stood in the kitchen of our small apartment, listening to the muffled sound of Leo crying on the other side of his bedroom door, and felt something hard and cold settle in my chest.

Leo's sobs went quiet, but the silence that followed felt worse.

Through the apartment walls, I could hear the next-door TV blaring some late-night movie, the sound of other people living ordinary lives while mine fractured into pieces.

Chapter Ten

Death and the Promise Broken

WINTER 2010–2011

The pressure started in March, right after word got out that I'd been offered an interview for the Ohio State scholarship. Within days, the whole extended family had opinions about what it meant.

"Olivia's planning to abandon her family right when they need her most," Aunt Patricia said during one of our rare family gatherings, her voice sharp as a knife. "Running off to college while her father is dying and her brother struggles with addiction."

"She's just a kid," Uncle Mike shot back. "She has the right to build her own life."

"She's seventeen years old," Aunt Patricia argued, "and the smartest person in this family. Leo looks up to her. Linda depends on her. And Bob... Bob's always been proudest of her achievements. Doesn't she owe them something?"

I sat at the kitchen table while they debated my future as if I wasn't there. Each word added to the weight I already carried, pressing down on my chest until I could barely breathe.

"What would you have her do?" Uncle Mike asked. "Stay here and drown in everyone else's crises? Sacrifice her life and education so she can enable Leo's drinking and Bob's dying?"

"I'd have her remember that family comes first," Aunt Patricia said. "That some things matter more than ambition."

"Like what?"

"Like being there when your father takes his last breath. Like helping your mother survive the worst period of her life. Like being the steady example her younger brother desperately needs."

Each point landed like a punch. Because they weren't wrong. I was planning to leave right when everything at home was collapsing. But I was also seventeen, and staying felt like volunteering to go under with them.

"Maybe Olivia could defer enrollment for a year," Cousin Janet offered. "Get Bob into hospice, help Leo into treatment, make sure Linda has support."

"And then defer again the next year?" Uncle Mike snapped. "And the year after that? When does Olivia get to live her own life?"

"When her family doesn't need her anymore."

"Her family will always need her. That's how dysfunction works. There's always another emergency. Always another reason why the responsible one can't leave."

I excused myself and stepped outside onto Uncle Mike's porch, the night air sharp in my lungs. Maybe they were right. Maybe choosing myself was selfish. Maybe my grades and scholarships meant nothing if they were built on leaving behind the people who needed me most.

But maybe staying would just keep everyone stuck. Maybe if I stayed, Leo wouldn't have to get sober because I'd clean up the fallout. Maybe Mommy wouldn't set boundaries because I'd step in. Maybe Daddy could keep drinking because I'd still be there to show up at the hospital.

At seventeen, I was realizing that no matter what choice I made, I was betraying someone.

The scholarship interview almost fell apart before it began.

I was supposed to be on Ohio State's campus at two o'clock sharp, sitting in front of professors who would decide whether I got the full ride. The only way I could afford to actually go. Instead, I was in Cleveland Metro's ICU at one-thirty, staring through a window at my father's unconscious body.

"You need to go," Uncle Mike told me in the waiting room, where I'd been sitting for six hours.

"I can't leave while he's unconscious. What if he wakes up and asks for me?"

"Olivia, this scholarship is your future. Bob would want you to go."

"How do you know what he'd want? He's unconscious."

"Because when he's sober, all he talks about is how proud he is of you. How you're going to be the one Parker who makes it out."

I looked at Daddy through the glass. Tubes. Machines. His skin yellow with jaundice. The body of a man losing the only fight that had ever really mattered.

"What if this is the last time I see him alive?" I whispered.

"Then you'll have missed a scholarship interview to sit in a hospital room. Is that the choice you want to make?"

The drive to Columbus took almost two hours, and I spent every mile fighting the urge to turn around. By the time I parked on campus, I had fifteen minutes to find the building, fix myself up, and somehow shift from crisis manager to scholarship candidate.

The reflection in the glass doors stopped me cold. My one good dress was wrinkled from the drive. My hair was a mess from raking my hands through it all morning. My eyes were red and swollen from crying. I looked exactly like what I was: a girl who'd spent the last day in a hospital waiting room.

"Miss Parker?" Dr. Williams, the committee chair, greeted me with the kind of warmth reserved for top applicants. "We're so pleased to meet you. Your application materials are very impressive."

"Thank you for this opportunity," I said, my voice steadier than I felt.

The panel sat behind a long table. Dr. Williams in the center, kind eyes and graying hair. To her left, a younger professor with glasses who smiled encouragingly. To her right, an older man with sharp eyes and crossed arms. Dr. Mars, according to his nameplate. He hadn't smiled once.

"Tell us about your goals," Dr. Williams asked. "What do you hope to accomplish here?"

I launched into the answer I'd rehearsed: career plans, research, leadership. But halfway through, my phone buzzed in my purse. Hospital.

My father.

"I'm sorry," I stammered, my mind splintering. "Could you... could you repeat the question?"

"We were asking about your leadership experience," Dr. Williams said gently. "Your academics speak for themselves. But tell us. Who are you outside the classroom?"

Leadership experience. Extracurriculars. They wanted to hear about debate teams and student councils, but how could I tell them that my "extracurriculars" were late-night ER visits, police calls, and twenty hours a week at Morrison's Grocery just to keep food on the table? That my "leadership" was holding my family together while the adults crumbled?

"I work part-time at Morrison's Grocery," I said finally, my voice tight. "And I help manage my family's challenges."

"What kind of challenges?" the younger professor asked, leaning forward.

The words felt like a trap. If I told the truth... addiction, arrests, poverty, my brother's drinking, my father's dying liver...

I'd look like a liability. But if I lied, I'd erase the very thing that had shaped every part of my life.

"Family health issues," I said, forcing my face to stay calm. "My father's dealing with some serious medical problems."

"I'm sorry to hear that. And you've maintained a perfect GPA while helping with that?"

"Yes."

"That demonstrates remarkable resilience and time management," Dr. Williams said. "Exactly the kind of character we're looking for."

I nodded, trying to sound more confident than I felt. My phone buzzed again in my purse. I ignored it.

Dr. Mars uncrossed his arms and leaned forward. His voice was flat, clinical. "Miss Parker, I want to address something directly. Your application is impressive. But I'm concerned about risk."

The room went cold.

"What kind of risk?" I asked.

"Students from unstable home environments often struggle with the transition to university life. The stress compounds. Grades drop. They withdraw." He tapped his pen against his notepad. "You've clearly overcome significant obstacles, but statistics show that students in crisis situations are more likely to fail out, especially in their first year."

My chest tightened. This was it. The moment they decided I was too damaged, too risky, too much of a liability.

"With all due respect," I said slowly, my voice steadier than I felt, "I understand your concern. But I think you're looking at this backward."

Dr. Mars raised an eyebrow. "How so?"

"You're worried that coming from chaos makes me fragile. But I've been managing crisis my entire life. I've held down a job, maintained perfect grades, and kept my family functioning while most students my age are figuring out how to do their own laundry." I paused, making sure my voice didn't shake. "The transition to college won't be harder for me. It'll be easier. Because for the first time, the only person I'll be responsible for is myself."

The younger professor nodded slightly. Dr. Williams was watching me closely.

"That's a nice theory," Dr. Mars said. "But theory and practice are different things. What happens when your father's condition worsens? When the next family emergency pulls you away mid-semester?"

The question was designed to corner me. To make me admit I'd always be divided, always one crisis away from falling apart.

But he was wrong.

"Then I'll handle it the same way I've handled every other emergency," I said. "By prioritizing what I can control and setting boundaries around what I can't. My family's dysfunction isn't going to disappear when I leave for college. But my ability to build something better will disappear if I don't go."

"That sounds like you're planning to abandon them," Dr. Mars said.

"No. It sounds like I'm planning to save myself so I can actually help them instead of drowning with them." My voice was sharp now, all the rehearsed politeness stripped away. "You want to know why I'm low-risk? Because I've spent seventeen years learning how to function under pressure in ways most people can't imagine. I've learned to compartmentalize, to budget time, to make impossible choices. Those aren't weaknesses. They're survival skills that will make me better at this than students who've never had to fight for anything."

The room was silent. Dr. Mars was still watching me, but something in his expression had shifted.

"And what happens when those survival skills aren't enough?" he asked quietly. "When the pressure becomes too much?"

For a moment, I saw it clearly. The rabbit under the oak tree, small and still, its eyes glassy with death. I'd been six years old, standing over it with no idea how to make things better, knowing only that some things couldn't be fixed no matter how hard you tried.

"Then I'll ask for help," I said. "Because I've also learned that pretending everything's fine doesn't work. The students who fail out are the ones who hide their struggles until it's too late. I won't do that. I can't afford to."

Dr. Williams exchanged a glance with the younger professor. Dr. Mars sat back, his pen still.

"One last question," Dr. Williams said. "Where do you see yourself in ten years?"

Ten years. Twenty-seven. I should have given them the safe answer about climbing some career ladder or managing teams in a corporate office. But my phone was buzzing in my purse with updates from the ICU, and pretending felt impossible.

"Ten years from now," I said quietly, "I want to be someone who broke a cycle. Someone whose kids grow up never wondering if there's enough money for groceries. Never feeling like they have to fix problems that aren't theirs to fix. I want them to be children, not caretakers."

Dr. Williams nodded slowly.

"I come from a family where addiction gets passed down like an heirloom," I continued. "Where being the responsible kid meant becoming the crisis manager before I could drive. My father is dying right now because he couldn't imagine a different life. And if I don't go to college, if I don't prove there's another way, then I'm just confirming what my family already believes. That people like us don't get out."

The silence that followed felt heavier than before.

"Thank you for your honesty, Miss Parker," Dr. Williams said finally. "We'll be in touch within two weeks."

I walked back to my car not knowing if I'd just saved my chances or destroyed them. But for the first time in the interview, I'd shown them who I really was. Not the perfect student they expected, but the one they were actually getting.

The drive back to Cleveland felt like moving between two worlds. One where fighting back might finally set me free, and another where it might cost me everything.

The email came on a Tuesday morning in late March while I sat at our chipped kitchen table trying to choke down soggy cornflakes. Mommy was getting ready for another double shift, moving through the apartment in her loose diner uniform that seemed to hang off her frame more each week. The place smelled like her too-strong coffee mixed with vanilla body spray, that combination that always reminded me of survival. Cheap perfume covering exhaustion.

My phone buzzed against the scratched Formica.

Subject line: Ohio State University Honors Program Admission Decision.

My stomach dropped like I'd swallowed a stone. This was it. The rejection I'd been bracing for ever since Dr. Mars challenged me, ever since I'd snapped at him instead of staying polite, ever since I'd let them see exactly how damaged and desperate I really was.

My fingers shook so badly I almost dropped the phone. I opened the email, the words swimming until I blinked hard.

Dear Miss Parker,

Congratulations! We are pleased to inform you that you have been selected as a recipient of our Full Merit Scholarship...

I read it once. Twice. A third time, the letters blurring with tears I didn't even feel coming. Full scholarship. Tuition, room, board, books. Everything. Four years. Paid for.

A sound tore out of me. Half sob, half laugh, and suddenly I couldn't catch my breath. The phone trembled in my hands as tears streaked down my face. Every sleepless night, every shift at Morrison's until my legs ached, every time I chose homework over a social life, every crisis I managed while still chasing perfect grades. It had all led here. It had worked.

"What is it, sweetheart?" Mommy asked, sharp with concern, her hairbrush clattering against the counter.

I looked up, tears streaming, and could barely whisper. "I got it. The full scholarship. Ohio State."

Her coffee mug slipped into the sink with a loud clatter. We just stared at each other across the cramped kitchen. She was there with tired eyes and half-pinned hair, and I was clutching the phone like it was the only solid thing in the world.

Then her face broke into the purest smile I'd ever seen, joy bright enough to burn through years of exhaustion. She rushed to me, wrapped me in her arms, both of us sobbing. She smelled like diner grease and vanilla and the harsh soap that cracked her hands from too many shifts.

"Oh, Olivia," she whispered into my hair. "I'm so proud of you. So incredibly proud."

I buried my face in her shoulder, feeling Grandpa's compass press against my leg through my pocket. North. Always north. And somehow it had led me here. To this moment, this way out.

But even as the relief poured through me, a heaviness settled in too. Because winning this meant leaving her behind. Leaving her with Leo's unraveling addiction. Leaving her to sit by Daddy's hospital bed as he slipped further away.

That afternoon, still clutching my phone like a lifeline, Uncle Mike called. His voice was flat, stripped of everything but truth.

"Liver failure. The doctors think days, not months."

I drove back to Cleveland Metro with the scholarship email still glowing on my phone, but it already felt like it belonged to someone else. My backpack carried printouts of a future that seemed a million miles away. My pocket carried Grandpa's compass, its weight pressing into my leg. And my chest carried the truth I could barely name: I was walking into a hospital to lose my father.

The ICU smelled like disinfectant and endings. Daddy looked swallowed by the bed, dwarfed by machines that kept count of every failing function. Gauze wrapped his head from the latest fall. His skin had gone the yellow of old butter. Even unconscious, his fingers twitched like they were still reaching for bottles.

When his eyes finally opened and found me, I almost didn't recognize them. For the first time in years, they were clear. My real father surfaced through the haze of disease just long enough to see me.

"Princess," he breathed, and even with tubes in his nose and mouth, his whole face lit up. Pride and joy cut through all the wreckage. "You came."

"Of course I came, Daddy." My voice cracked. I dragged the plastic chair right up to his bed, so close I could smell the sour cocktail of medicine and the faint sweetness of a body shutting down.

"Uncle Mike... told me." Each word cost him. His chest heaved with the effort. "Ohio State."

"Yes, Daddy. Full scholarship."

His eyes welled up. "So... proud." The words came out broken, his breath rattling between them. "My... princess."

"Thank you, Daddy."

He closed his eyes, gathering strength. When they opened again, something urgent flickered there.

"Stories," he whispered. "Green Eggs…"

"Green Eggs and Ham," I finished, already crying. "I remember."

"You… in my lap." His hand searched until it found mine. The fingers that once felt unshakable were paper-thin and ice-cold. "Strawberry… shampoo."

He was trying to tell me something, piecing it together word by word, breath by breath. I leaned closer.

"Best… moments… in my life." His voice was barely there now. "Not money. Just… you. Questions about… Sam."

I squeezed his hand, terrified of how fragile it felt. "I remember, Daddy. I remember all of it."

His breathing grew more labored. He struggled to say something else, his mouth forming shapes I couldn't quite make out.

"Daddy, save your strength—"

"No." The word came out fierce despite its weakness. "Important."

I waited, my heart pounding.

"Sorry," he finally managed. "So… sorry, princess."

"For what?"

His face twisted with the effort of getting it out. "Plates. Scared you. Made you... hide."

"Daddy, you don't have to—"

"Sickness." He tapped his chest weakly with one finger. "Not... me. The real... me... loved you. More than..."

He couldn't finish. His breathing was too hard now, each inhale a visible struggle.

"I know," I said, tears streaming. "I know, Daddy. I love you, too."

"More than... all the stars... in the sky." The words came out in pieces, barely audible.

Our old bedtime phrase. It cut through everything (the machines, the jaundice, the years of chaos) landing in me like both a blessing and a goodbye.

His eyes closed. Opened again with effort. Fear flickered there now, mixed with something else. Something he was trying desperately to say.

"Leo," he whispered.

My chest tightened.

"Same... pull." His hand squeezed mine with what little strength remained. "See it... in him."

"I know."

"Don't... leave him." Each word was agony. "Promise."

"Daddy—"

"Promise… you'll… love him. Even when…" He couldn't finish. The machines beeped faster. His breathing turned ragged.

"I promise," I said through tears. "I'll go to school. But I won't disappear. I'll love him even when it hurts."

"Good." His voice was almost gone now. "Good… girl."

Then his hand went slack in mine. His eyes closed. And the machines kept breathing for him while I sat there, holding on, knowing these were his last moments.

The words he'd given me were broken, scattered, hard to piece together. But I understood. Underneath the fragments was everything he'd wanted to say. That he loved me. That he was sorry. That he was afraid of what would happen to Leo without me.

I pressed my face into his shoulder and sobbed, breathing in medicine and mortality and the faint trace of Old Spice he used to wear when he wanted so badly to be the man we needed.

The monitor's beeping filled the silence until suddenly it didn't. A stutter, then slow, uneven tones. Then nothing.

Silence.

The flatline cut through the ICU like a scream. Nurses and doctors rushed past me, their movements a blur of practiced urgency.

This was it. The moment I'd feared and rehearsed in my head since childhood: my father dying while I held proof in my pocket that I could finally leave this place.

For ninety suspended seconds, I stood in that hallway with the compass burning in my hand, caught between the six-year-old who vowed never to become him and the seventeen-year-old who'd just promised not to sacrifice herself for anyone else.

"Time of death, 4:47 PM," the doctor said quietly, stepping out with that look professionals wear when they've acknowledged a fight they knew was unwinnable.

He was gone.

Bob Parker was gone. The father who made me laugh with silly voices, who gave me his father's compass, who taught me that love could exist alongside fear.

And my first emotion wasn't grief.

It was relief.

Relief that it was finally over and that I wouldn't have to balance my scholarship against his dying anymore. Relief that

I could walk toward Ohio State without wondering if he was drinking himself into oblivion while I was gone.

The thought formed fully before I could stop it: I wanted my father to die so I could be free.

The shame of it burned hot, but the honesty of it weighed heavier.

"Would you like a few minutes alone with him?" the nurse asked softly.

"Yes," I said, my voice barely there. "Yes, please."

He lay so still on the hospital bed, stripped of the tubes and machines that had kept him alive for those last hours. Without the wires and noise, he looked smaller than I remembered. Peaceful, even. No pain etched across his forehead. No desperation twisting his mouth. No trembling hands reaching for a bottle that was never enough.

For the first time, I saw what he might have been without the disease. The man addiction stole from us one drink at a time.

"I'm sorry," I whispered, my voice catching. "I'm so sorry, Dad. I felt relieved. I wanted you gone so I could be free. I'm sorry."

But apologies couldn't rewind the moment in the hallway when his death felt like liberation instead of loss. The thought had come, clean and sharp, and once it existed, I couldn't make it un-exist.

Maybe Leo was right all along about me being selfish.

The realization hit cold. I had spent my whole life swearing I was different, better than the Parker men who drank themselves into oblivion, stronger than the chaos I grew up in. But when it mattered most, when my father's life hung in the balance, I revealed something ugly.

I wanted him dead.

Not because I didn't love him. I did. But loving him had been exhausting. Watching him drink himself to death had drained me dry. His death meant I could finally stop carrying a burden that was never mine to bear.

And what kind of daughter feels relief when her father dies? What kind of monster does that make me?

I sat there for twenty minutes beside his body, willing myself to feel the right kind of grief. I cried, yes, but underneath the tears was something worse than sadness. A coldness.

"Olivia?" Uncle Mike's voice broke the silence. He stood in the doorway, his face worn with grief.

"I'm okay," I lied. Because how could I tell him the truth? That I wasn't shattered the way I should have been, that I was horrified by my own relief more than by our father's death?

"Your mother's on her way. Leo's here too. He's in the bathroom, throwing up. The shock hit him hard."

Leo was on the floor sick with grief while I sat next to Daddy's body calmly cataloging my emotions, terrified by my own numbness.

Two hours later, I left Cleveland Metro Hospital with a plastic bag of Daddy's belongings in one hand and the scholarship email glowing on my phone in the other.

Bob Parker was dead at forty-five, his liver destroyed by fifteen years of drinking.

Olivia Parker was bound for Ohio State with a full scholarship, her escape route confirmed.

In the parking lot, I caught my reflection in a car window. I looked... appropriate. Sad but composed, the way a seventeen-year-old was supposed to look when her father had just died. But in my eyes, I saw something that chilled me. The same distance I'd seen in him. The same ability to disconnect when things got too heavy to hold.

I had spent my life building walls to protect myself from his disease. Now I wondered if those walls had turned me into someone who could feel relief at her father's death. Someone closer to Bob Parker than I'd ever wanted to admit.

The scholarship felt heavier than ever as Uncle Mike drove us back through Millfield, past the streets where I'd learned too early that love could look like poison and that promises made in fear rarely survived the test of real life.

Three days later, we buried Bob Parker under a gray April sky. The heavy clouds felt right, like the world had chosen the perfect backdrop for ending a life marked by pain, sickness, and the slow damage of addiction.

I stood between Mommy and Leo, staring at the plain wooden casket as it sank into the ground. Inside it lay the man who'd given me Grandpa's compass, who'd taught me that love and hurt could exist in the same breath. The crowd was small: Uncle Mike, a handful of cousins, a couple of men from the gas station where Daddy had worked during one of his brief sober streaks, and Mrs. Kowalski, Richard's widow, who'd driven two hours just to stand graveside.

"He tried," she told me afterward, her hands warm on my shoulders. "Richard always said your father tried harder than most people ever do. Sometimes trying is all we can ask."

I nodded and thanked her. But inside, I wondered if trying counted when it never once saved him. Or us.

Leo cried through the whole service. Deep, body-shaking sobs that seemed too big for his fifteen-year-old frame. He looked smaller too, like the grief had stripped weight from him along with hope. His clothes hung loose on him, and there were dark hollows under his eyes.

"I should have been there more," he whispered when the first shovelful of dirt hit the coffin. "I should've gone home from Uncle Mike's on weekends. Maybe if he knew I still believed in him..."

"Leo, no. This wasn't your fault."

"Then whose was it?" His voice cracked. "Somebody has to be responsible for him dying alone."

I wanted to tell him no child carries that weight. That this was the disease, not him. But at that graveside, with Leo looking at me like I might have an answer, the words just wouldn't come.

Mommy was quiet through it all, her hand wrapped around Leo's, her tears steady but silent. When the pastor asked if anyone wanted to share, she shook her head and pulled my brother close.

Later, back at Uncle Mike's house, the cousins filled the kitchen with talk about weather and football and work. Anything but Bob Parker. Mommy sat at the table, her face pale, her voice cutting through the small talk.

"I keep thinking about Green Eggs and Ham," she said suddenly. "He did the voices. Made Sam-I-Am sound like a little boy, and the other one grumpy. Olivia used to giggle so hard she'd hiccup."

"He was good with stories," Uncle Mike said softly.

"He wanted to be a good father. He really did. He just..." She stopped.

"He just couldn't beat the disease," Uncle Mike finished for her. "That doesn't make him bad. That makes him sick."

I listened to them circle the memories, polishing the good parts while skirting the wreckage. Their grief looked normal, clean. Mine didn't. Mine was complicated, laced with guilt and relief, wrong in ways I couldn't admit out loud.

I should have been crying for the man who'd read me bedtime stories, who taught me to drive in the Kmart parking lot, who gave me his compass like a blessing. Instead, I was thinking about the acceptance letter in my backpack, about the orientation packet for a future that had nothing to do with Millfield.

That night, the house emptied out, leaving just the three of us. I sat on the edge of the guest bed, Grandpa's compass in my hands. The brass was cool, worn smooth from years of worry and use. The needle swung, then stilled, steady as always.

I thought of the promise I'd made on a bathroom floor when I was six. *Dear God, I will never, ever, EVER be like my father. I will never drink. I will never hurt people. I will never make my children scared.* That vow had built the scaffolding of my life. For eleven years, it was what set me apart from him.

I tucked the compass into my pocket, lay down, and pulled the blanket to my chin. The house was quiet. The kind of quiet I'd been waiting for my entire life.

And in that silence, I felt something new.

Freedom. Even if it came with a weight I wasn't sure I'd ever stop carrying.

Three years later, I stood in my dorm room at Ohio State, staring at the McKinsey Consulting firm interview invitation letter on my desk. Final round interview. Chicago office. Everything I'd been working toward since I was six years old.

The campus outside my window looked like a postcard. Spring semester, senior year. Summa cum laude almost guaranteed. The life I'd promised myself was finally here.

My phone buzzed.

Leo.

I glanced at the screen, then at my economics textbook open on the bed. Thesis revisions due tomorrow. Study group in an hour. Interview prep after that.

Whatever Leo needed could wait.

I sent the call to voicemail and turned back to my work, unaware that my brother was hiding in an abandoned building on the east side of Millfield, his hands shaking as footsteps echoed outside.

Not knowing he had six weeks left to live.

Not knowing that the promise I'd made at Daddy's deathbed... to watch over Leo, to never disappear... was already breaking.

The phone buzzed again. Another call.

I silenced it and kept reading, the compass heavy in my pocket, its needle pointing north toward a future I thought I'd earned.

Behind me, Leo's name lit up my screen one more time, then went dark.

Chapter Eleven

Author's Note

THANK YOU VERY MUCH for spending time with Book 1, ***Never Like My Father***, in the five-book saga ***The Daughter of a Drunk***.

If Olivia's story hit you, please consider leaving a quick review on Amazon. Even two sentences help other people like us find this book.

But Olivia's story isn't over.

Book 1 was about trying not to become my father. Book 2, ***Exactly Like My Father***, is about what happens when Olivia realizes she already has.

She thinks she's broken the cycle. She's wrong.

You can find Book 2 online, so don't wait. Just search "***Exactly Like Your Father by Howard Kane***" wherever you buy books.

Thank you for reading.

With gratitude,

Howard Kane

232

This page was intentionally left blank.

233

This page was intentionally left blank.

234

This page was intentionally left blank.

This page was intentionally left blank.

236

This page was intentionally left blank.

www.ingramcontent.com/pod-product-compliance
Lightning Source LLC
Chambersburg PA
CBHW061248310726
48971CB00007B/2269